GIFTED

GIFTED

THE SPYCE CHRONICLES

L. SUTTON

ARCHWAY
PUBLISHING

Archway Publishing books may be ordered through booksellers or by contacting:

Archway Publishing
1663 Liberty Drive
Bloomington, IN 47403
www.archwaypublishing.com
844-669-3957

ISBN: 978-1-6657-3447-9 (sc)
ISBN: 978-1-6657-3472-1 (e)

Library of Congress Control Number: 2022922459

Print information available on the last page.

Archway Publishing rev. date: 12/09/2022

Great, it's morning and I still haven't slept. Another all-night rendezvous with a book that was just too intriguing to put down. Whoever wrote this must have spent most of their time alone. Not just as a social outcast, but they obviously did not have any siblings, either. To hate the world with such passion should be commemorated. Every soul feels tortured at some point; just some are more than others. I do not think my life is so bad that I could ever commit a murder or suicide, not to say that I would not mind torturing a few people. I would not do it physically, just mentally. Since that is what they do to me. For example, my professor, Professor Steinman, he always tells us to do our best, but, when I did my best on my theory of evolution and natural selection research paper. My best exceeded his expectations. Now I am being accused of cheating. He wants me to show my research. It would not bother me so much if I had any research to show. Unfortunately, I do not. I have never taken notes. There has never been a need for me to do so. All my research is ten years old from a journal that I found in my father's study. The research was his own.

My memory is impeccable. I can remember books I read in the third-grade cover to cover, word for word. I do not know how, but I can remember everything perceptibly. Some would call it a photographic memory, some say eidetic memory. It is common, just not of this magnitude. My IQ can not be measured on traditional test it exceeds the max of two hundred. My capacity for knowledge made me want to learn as many things as possible. My competitive nature caused me to strive to be the best, but humbly. I remember when I was three years old; my mom had left my siblings and me with my dad while she was out of town. My dad had some of his friends over. I'm guessing that my mom was oblivious to the situation. I don't think my mother would concede to such ostentatious women in her home, or worse, bedroom, while she was away. Well, at three years old, I could see no fault. To me, they were just daddy's friends. When I was twelve, my father told me he would take me to a seminar that I waited for two months to go to. He later rescinded the offer. He claimed he had an important meeting; it was normal for him to flake and disappear. I was so upset and frustrated that I went straight to my mom and told her everything that I saw when I was three. My father, of course, claimed that I fabricated the entire story. He claimed that my anger enhanced my over-the-top imagination. So, to prove to my mother I was being sincere, I gave her one woman's full name, identification number and address (which was in the purse they left me alone with). My mother soon after hired a private investigator. She learned my tale was not fiction, but indeed real. Apparently, my father was still meeting with said woman. They separated for two years and right before they were ready to reconcile, my dad disappeared. After being missing for five years, my mom had him declared deceased. The guilt of these events still weighs heavily on my psyche.

Now, I am on my way to the Dean's office. I am sure he knows I did not cheat on my research paper; coincidentally, he had married my mom the previous year. Yeah, I know annoying but useful, especially now. Primarily because I do not have an appointment and I do not want to wait two weeks for one. "Good morning Ms. Grace." I kindly said to the receptionist. She smiled at me and then replied.

"Good morning Ms. Spyce, Dean Drako is expecting you." My stepfather comes from money, just like my mother. Only difference is he is an only child. It shows in his office, or as I like to call it, his Grecian throne room. He has statues, pottery, and plants everywhere. The color scheme is white and gold.

"Hello Ignatios, how is your day going?" I asked politely.

"Have a seat Shontelle." He replied with an obvious restraint. He does not muse the idea of me using his first name at school. Just as I loathe calling him Dean Drako. It sounds too much like an evil villain from a comic book or cartoon.

He sat behind a Carrera white marble desk in a soft, white leather chair. He looked up at me. Something, possibly the file lying in front of him on his desk, disturbed him. It must be mine. "Your mother worries about you." He said with scrutiny in his voice.

"Ignatios, you know I wouldn't..." I started.

"Not about that." He interrupted. "We know you didn't cheat on your assignment. With a memory and an IQ like yours, you would not need to. No, this is about your social interactions."

I just stared at him, confused for a moment, then I said. "I don't have problems with anyone, from what I can recall. I rarely even talk to people."

He sighed heavily. "That's the problem. You don't socialize with anyone and you don't have a friend in the world."

"I have friends. I'm very cordial." I replied defensively.

The look he gave me was cynical. "Just because you know someone's name does not categorize them as your friend. With that said, your mother wants you to come over next weekend. She is having a party. She wants you to give out these invitations to your friends or any acquaintances." His tone was flat with a hint of command.

"What if I don't want to go?" I asked calmly.

"Please, just try. Your mom just wants what's best for you. We both do. If you need anything, just let us know." He said with sincerity and something else in his voice, hope maybe.

"I might have to bribe some people, but I will do what I can." I said with a hint of sarcasm.

He smiled at me, then said, "I'll take that."

"Goodbye Ignatios. I'll see you later." I said as I walked out of his throne room. I left with haste, just in case he forgot something like my rent-a-friend. In my haste to leave, I walked the wrong way down the corridor. I spun around to go the other way. I ran into something that felt like a human textured statue. I almost fell straight back, but something kept me a float.

2

"I'm so sorry, are you alright?" I heard a prodigious tenor voice say,

"It's okay, I'm fine, and I should pay better attention to my surroundings." I exclaimed with my head down. I was afraid to look up and see that I ran into Zeus himself.

"Hey, I'm Adrian." He announced.

My head shot up a bit too quickly and introduced its self to his chin.

"I am such a klutz. Are you okay?" I asked apologetically.

"Yes, I'm fine." He replied, trying to restrain his agony,

"Are you sure?" I asked, hoping he could see the empathy in my eyes.

He looked me in the eye and smiled. "Yes, I'm okay. Don't worry about it. Accidents happen."

"I'm Shontelle, the train that just hit you," I told him bashfully.

"I know who you are. I've been your brother's best friend since I lived next door to your family when I was nine." He informed me.

"Really, I've never noticed someone that looked like you before." The minute the words were out, I wanted to take them back.

"I believe that since your attention seemed to always be preoccupied by a book. The way you focused in on each page made me interested." He teased, the humor clear in his voice. I wish I had adverted my eyes from that book a lot sooner. To detect His presence alone would have been a blessing. He is the epitome of a beautiful man. Tall, ripped and handsome and that's me putting it lightly. He has dark blonde hair, light green eyes, smooth creamy ivory skin, a goatee with the same shade of blonde, along with a few random strands of red blended in, and two perfectly seductive lips that were beckoning mine towards him. He must be well over six feet tall, with the body of a Roman Gladiator. I stood there, bewildered.

"Would you like to come to a party, it's next weekend? It's the least I can do after… well, you know." I asked frantically, my words tied to my tongue. He took a step towards me.

"Sure, that sounds nice." He smiled. It was as beautiful as a beach front sunrise.

"You can bring a friend if you like." I told him as I reached out to hand him an invitation. Although I really hope he comes alone, I definitely want him for myself.

"Well, Brandon has already given me an invitation, but now I'll definitely show up." He grinned provocatively. I could feel the blood rushing to my head. Please do not let me pass out.

"I can't believe you're Brandon's best friend. The only person I remember seeing him with was this dorky little boy that always had this ugly rat with him." I told him, smirking, tickled by the thought.

"That was me." He proclaimed. My face dropped at that moment. I'm surprised I didn't just hit the floor. I seriously need to punch myself in the face. I looked at him apologetically.

"Don't worry about it. We all do strange things as kids. I believe I can recall a cute little girl whom went into a full-on panic when her teddy bear fell into the pool. I believe you spent at least twenty minutes trying to resuscitate that bear." He said in a teasing tone.

"I had remembered reading that you're not supposed to stop CPR on a drowning victim until help arrives." I told him, giggling softly.

"Would you like an escort to your next class?" He asked. I instantly regretted not having an early morning lecture.

"No, thank you." I said. He looked surprised, and then as I registered what had just happened, he was turning to walk away. I cut off his imminent departure.

"I mean, I don't have any morning classes, but I can walk you to your class if you would like?" He smiled to reassure me and then said.

"We're already here; I help around in the office on most Mondays, maybe next time. I'll see you around?" I nodded at him, then walked away. I could feel those beautiful green eyes staring into my back. I desperately wanted to turn around and get one more long look at one of the most perfect specimens of a man on this planet. Instead, I opted to continue my way off campus back to my condo.

I walked into my place so distorted; that I walked right into someone that was dripping wet and wearing a towel wrapped around his waist. What in the world is going on today? Can I expect to keep running into random, sexy as hell men today? This seductive man looked at me with a wide, sexy grin and perusing eyes.

"Hello gorgeous." His voice was deep, sensual, and alluring. I stood there shell-shocked until suddenly a familiar face appeared out of the kitchen. My roommate that is supposed to be taking this semester off, Dahlia. Her long, jet black hair flowed around her petite frame in silky, loose curls. Her radiant, normally golden skin is almost copper now. Although some would consider her to be 'fun size' at five feet three inches, she has a huge fun and outgoing personality. Just don't get on her bad side. I've seen her make some of the most arrogant meat heads cry just from one conversation.

"Dahlia, what are you doing here? I thought you were touring Europe with your family this semester?" I asked as I walked towards her and away from the Arabian Prince.

"Well, thanks to a certain philanderer, our trip had to be cut short. He didn't notice that the last woman he defiled was wearing a wedding band. To make a long story short, the woman's husband noticed him kissing her as she was leaving his suite." She said as she gave a disapproving look over my shoulder to the man behind me.

I turned around to look at said philanderer. "Are you her twin brother Dorian, the famous ladies' man?" Now why did I have to say that?

"Is that what she told you?" He asked with a cunning smirk on his insanely beautiful face. "Trust me when I say she exaggerates, although she did not exaggerate your beauty. She was quite modest. You are exquisite." My lashes fluttered at the compliment.

"Give it a rest Dorian; trust me, she is way too intelligent to waste her time on someone like you." Dahlia said as she gave me a contrite look. I smiled at her before making my way to my room. Dorian was still standing in the center of the living space in just a towel, and water covering his illustrious and captivating body. He obviously wasn't shy. Why would he be with those perfect abs and defined shoulders? His arms were thicker than both of mine put together. A slow throbbing in my pelvis was my hint to get away from him and his powerful allure. Dahlia followed me, Dorian trailing behind her; I sat on the edge of my bed and began removing my shoes.

Dahlia hesitated in the doorway before she spoke. "Spyce I need to ask you a favor."

"Sure, what is it?" I asked.

"Do you think it would be alright if Dorian stayed with us this semester? He unfortunately leased out his townhouse for the semester. I know the last thing he wants to do is stay with our parents at their house." I now understand her hesitance. She knows how uncomfortable I can get around strangers.

"Can't he stay in a hotel?" I asked softly, avoiding eye contact with the person in question that is standing quietly behind her, still only wearing a towel and water droplets that were slowly cascading over his perfectly firm chest. His eyes locked on me, probably just waiting for my answer. I looked up to see that those eyes were looking for more than just an answer.

"I promise he will be on his best behavior." She nudged him on his side with her elbow. He held his hands up, giving her a look, feigning innocence.

I conceded. "Sure."

The family resemblance became more adamant when both Dahlia and Dorian smiled at me. "Thank you." They both said before they left me to myself, Dahlia quietly closing the door behind her.

An hour after I was home, I decided to skip my classes for the day. I mean, I've never missed a day since grade school. I think I'll be okay. Plus, I'll have my doctorates in less than two months, anyway. I heard a soft tap at my room door.

"Come in, it's not locked." I announced. Of course, mister fabulous would be at my door. Well, at least he's wearing clothes, not that it makes him look any less mouth watering. His taste in clothing is immaculate and black is definitely his color. His button down has three buttons he left open, showing off his smooth tanned skin underneath, accompanied by black fitted jeans that didn't hide his thick toned legs or perfect arse. His only accessory, a simple gold watch with a black leather band. He probably has a personal shopper. Like mine, Dahlia and Dorian's family have old money, she told me when we met my first year of grad school. Her parents are both heirs of an oil and silk empire, even though they're both scientists.

"Dahlia wanted to know if you would like to accompany us to The Lost Pattern." He asked as he seductively ate my strawberry gelato from the container. I can't tell if I'm frustrated from him eating my gelato or jealous of the spoon that gets to feel his tongue and those sexy lips. It's the latter, I'm sure, lucky damn spoon.

"Can you thank her for the invitation, but I think I'll stay in for a while." I told him, trying to conceal my interest. I was getting a little irritated, mostly because of how flushed he made me.

"I will do that, but if you change your mind, you know where to find us." He exited out of my room. I flopped back on my pillow top mattress, trying to remember how to breathe. Reaching over to my nightstand, I turned on my own remixed rendition of Le Quattro Stagioni by Vivaldi. I laid there and tried to relax my mind. I don't understand what's happening to me right now.

To me, confusion is a foreign concept, but I am definitely confused. I have never seen myself as the girl that guys would find appealing. I have always seen myself as an outcast, a loner mostly. Most people ignored me and acted as if I were invisible, or at least for me. That's how it feels. I looked at my reflection in the full-length mirror on my wall. It's facing directly towards the base of my bed beside my bathroom door. A few of my midnight black curls fell out of my pinned updo along my brow and at the nape of my neck. My eyes are large and cat like silver-grey orbs. My normally light brown skin is now reddened from my summer exploits at the beach. My body is well toned thanks to my daily workouts and genetics, I'm sure, but mostly curvy towards my lower half. Small waist, thick hips and a more than plump ass. My breast over flow in my small hands, but would fit perfectly in Adrian or Dorian's big hands. What the hell, brain, are you malfunctioning? Back to my self-examination. My legs are long with thick thighs. I blame my father, a Nubian giant that towered over most people at six feet eight inches for my height of five feet ten inches. I think if my mother wasn't so petite, I would have been over six feet as well, like my brother. Looking down at my legs and then back into the mirror, I could almost imagine having them wrapped around Dorian's waist, or maybe Adrian's head. Flopping back on my bed, I tried to just lay there, clear my lust filled thoughts and just let the music run through me, relaxing my mind for a little while.

An hour later, I realized relaxation is out of the question. My stomach growled, reminding me that the English breakfast tea that I had this morning before my meeting, is not a breakfast. It's a little late for breakfast now. I got up and went into the kitchen. I guess I could make myself an omelet. I looked into the refrigerator to grab what ingredients I needed and noticed I was missing a few key ingredients. Such as milk, eggs and parsley. It also appears that I need some more strawberry gelato thanks to my new temporary roommate. I guess I'll be taking a trip to the market. I grabbed my wallet and keys, then I left out the door. Once I was in the hall, I realized my big brother Brandon, whom lives just upstairs, may have everything I need, since he is a four star critically acclaimed chef. I took the elevator up to his floor. Once I was outside his door, I knocked twice and there was no response. I turned and walked away. I had only taken a few steps when I heard the door open. To my astonishment, it was not Brandon whom opened the door, instead it was Adrian.

"Hello Shontelle." he said.

"What are you doing here?" I asked with a little too much excitement in my voice.

"I'm staying with Brandon for a few weeks while my place is under renovations." Adrian explained.

"Oh, well, I just stopped by to get a few things. Is Brandon here?" I asked, calmer.

"No, he's at the Lost Pattern. They had some type of emergency and he went to take care of it. Nothing serious." I assume he added the last part because of the look of concern that whisked over my face.

"Do you mind if I come in?" I asked.

"Of course not, come in. Where are my manners?" He stepped aside so I could enter Brandon's condo. The floor plan is identical to mine, but the furniture and decor couldn't be more different. While I wasn't exactly a minimalist, my place seemed basic compared to Brandon's couture decked out ambience. Brandon is actually very humble and frugal, which is why our eldest sister Julissa insisted on decorating for him.

"I'm just going to grab a few things out of the refrigerator." I walked into the kitchen.

"Hey, do you have any plans for this evening?" He asked.

"Why do you ask?" I asked idiotically. The lack of ingredients slightly distracted me in my dear brother's refrigerator. He obviously hasn't gone shopping for groceries either. "I mean no I don't." I said, flustered, as I turned around to face him. My breath caught at our proximity. Adrian definitely could consume me with his presence alone.

"Would you do me the honor of accompanying me to dinner tonight?" He was standing in between me and the pantry, staring at me quizzically.

"I would love to join you for dinner." I said in a whisper, afraid to breathe him in.

He stepped closer to me. I could smell his woodsy cinnamon scent. It took everything in me to keep my focus on his words and not start drooling like a starved dog. "So, I'll pick you up at eight o'clock tonight?"

"Eight is great." I could slap myself. I am such an idiot. He walked me to the door with his hand on my lower back and goosebumps spread from my neck to my bum.

"I'll see you tonight." I said, before making my hasty retreat.

"Until then." His reply was soft and almost distant behind me as I left.

What am I supposed to do now? I have not been on a date in years. My last date was my senior prom. I have never felt such dismay. This would be a good time to have a confidant. I really need someone to talk to. I know exactly who can help me and where I can find her.

3

I stood outside of the Lost Pattern, trying to establish what I wanted to say to Dahlia. This is absurd. I shouldn't have to ask my roommate for dating advice. Just as I turned to walk away, I heard someone calling out my last name.

"Spyce." There it is again.

Who is that? I looked back towards the lost pattern and saw Dorian walking towards me. I stood there mesmerized as I analyzed him with a little more interest. He is insanely attractive, like a gorgeous Egyptian warrior. He has thick, wavy, black hair that comes to his shoulders. Soul stealing hazel eyes, with long beautiful lashes. He had a perfectly prominent nose. His perfect, beckoning lips are my favorite of his features. They were extremely tantalizing. His body was very muscular and well chiseled for someone so lean. He wasn't as tall as Adrian, but still taller than me and perfectly built.

"Hello, do I have something on my face?" He asked with a concerned look as he approached me in front of my brother's restaurant.

"I'm sorry, um no you don't, and I was just looking for Dahlia." I quickly said, discombobulated by this walking sex doll.

"Well, she should join us momentarily. She just went to the restroom. We were actually on our way back." He told me with a glisten in his eyes. I can see why women are so drawn to him.

He has a wonderfully inviting essence around him. I feel almost compelled to do anything to keep his attention solely on me. What am I thinking? Guys like him are the exact reason I have lost all interest in dating. When I was in high school, Guys would ask me out and after only one date, I knew rather or not I would talk to them again. My attention to details made me notice all their flaws almost immediately. Not that I expect perfection, but some decorum at least. For example, one guy, Daniel Jacobs, had a nasty habit of putting his hands in the wrong places even after being told to stop. Not to mention how his eyes always seem to become instantly magnetized to every beautiful female he encounters. We can just say he was not my type. After the boys at my high school and my dad, I learned very early what men I shouldn't pursue romantically. College was different. I started early while I was still in high school. When I graduated from high school, I also graduated from college with a degree in organic chemistry. I have two Master degrees. I'm currently working on dual PHd's in biochemistry and microbiology. Which has left me too busy to socialize. I guess now that my thesis' are both complete and waiting for review, I'm free to do so. Despite what most people that know me think, I'm not still a virgin. I have had sex, but only the first time was worth it. I get urges just like any other red-blooded mammal and right now Dorian looks perfectly capable of helping me find release.

"Well, I'm glad I caught you guys. I really need to talk to Dahlia." I exclaimed as I looked down at the ground. Keeping my mind focused on my objective seems impossible every time I look at him.

"Perhaps I can be of some help. I would never want you to be left in need." Dorian's seductive baritone voice sounds piqued with interest. He is even cuter when he wants to help, crap! Yeah, I'm doomed. Just before I could reply, Dahlia came out of the restaurant. Making her way over to us.

"I'm here, I'm here." She announced as she quickly approached.

"Hey Spyce I'm glad you could make it but we were just on our way home."

"I actually would like to talk to you, if you have a few minutes to spare." I told her.

"Of course we can talk. I'll just ride back with you." Dahlia suggested.

"That would be perfect." I replied. She turned to Dorian and dangled her car keys in his face.

"Sure, sis, I'll drive your eco friendly electric race car home for you. See you guys back at the condo." Dorian said before he snatched the keys and walked across the street to her car.

"So, what's up?" Dahlia asked as we walked towards my car.

I waited until we both were inside of the car before responding.

"I guess I need your help with something I don't have that much positive experience with." I could feel my face heating with embarrassment.

"Something like what?" She asked, looking at me attentively after buckling her safety belt.

"I haven't been on a date in a very long time and I agreed to go out with this guy tonight." I rushed the words out.

"Oh, men, that is something I know plenty about." Dahlia said with a wicked smile.

"Well, the things I know about men are not good. I haven't had the privilege of dating a good guy. Therefore, that is why I'm coming to you. I don't want to run him off with all my bitter assumptions and accusations. So, are you willing to assist me?" I asked, hating that this conversation was even necessary.

"I'll do my best to help you. Although I think you'll be just fine being yourself. You have already gotten through the hard part." She said.

I raised my brow with curiosity. "What was the hard part?"

"Getting him to ask you out." She replied, "By the way, who

is the lucky guy? He must be ridiculously gorgeous." She said with exuberance in her voice.

"What makes you say that?" I asked.

"I see guys practically drooling over you and you act oblivious to their advances. He either identified your enigma or he is impossibly hot." she explained.

"I never knew guys even noticed me, let alone were drooling over me. I assumed everyone thinks that I'm strange." I was feeling more confused than appeased by this information.

"Shontelle, you're not strange. You are a gorgeous and insanely smart girl. Sometimes that makes people uncomfortable because you intimidate them. Don't let other people's weaknesses bring you down." She encouraged.

"Thank you." I said.

"For what?" she asked.

"For what you just said. Knowing you see me that way makes me feel good. You're a great friend." I said.

"Spyce we aren't just friends. We're best friends,We have been for a few years." Dahlia said with no doubt.

"Really? I thought we were just friendly roommates." I replied, heedless of that fact. Although she has always been kind to me, I always assumed Dahlia saw me as just an acquaintance.

"A friend is someone you trust. Someone whose company you enjoy and, as far as I can tell, I am the only person you associate with outside of your family. I rarely even see you with them, except maybe Brandon." She said the last part with a small grin.

I sighed. "I am glad you consider me your friend. The feeling is mutual."

"Best friend." She clarified.

"Right, best friend." I confirmed.

Once we were home, I noticed Dorian was still out, even though he parked Dahlia's car in her spot. Dahlia and I continued our conversation about tonight. I filled her in with all the information about Adrian and his relationship with my brother, Brandon. Turns out, she already knows him and apparently, he has asked her about me a few times before.

"Sometimes I'm so amaurotic I never notice the people that are around me." I said as I looked for my make-up case. Dahlia insisted I let her work her makeup magic on me for my date.

"I wouldn't say that. You are just really focused on your goals. Trust me, that is a great thing. Plus, you didn't seem to have any vision problems when you saw Adrian." She said. I blushed at that fact.

"That's because I crashed into him like a freight train. I thought I died when I saw him glowing like an archangel." We both laughed. A light tap at my door paused our conversation. Dorian stood in the doorway.

"I couldn't help but overhear you guys discussing an angel, so I felt it is only right that I be present during any conversations about me." He said with a sexy and devious smirk on his face.

"Trust me, no one would ever call you an angel. You're more like an incubus." Dahlia proclaimed. They both laughed mockingly at each other.

I interrupted their sarcastic banter. "Would you guys like to come to a party next weekend? It's at my parents' house." They both looked at me with awe. I have never seen Dahlia look so bewildered. "Can you guys please say something? You're making me vexed." I guess they noticed how disconcerted I was because they immediately snapped out of their temporary daze.

"I apologize for the momentary astonishment. I just never took you for a party, girl." Dahlia said, obviously still in awe.

"Your right. I'm not really into parties. My mom is, and she insisted I invite some friends or more like to make some friends to invite." I said with a half smile.

"I guess that makes more sense. Of course, I would love to come and support you. When is it?" she asked.

"A week from Saturday at seven, black tie attire, so dress your best." I handed her an invitation. I walked over to Dorian, whom was standing quietly in the doorway this whole time. I stood directly in front of him. I hadn't noticed just how tall he was until this moment. I knew he was taller than me, but I had to look up at him to look into those golden orbs of his. Maybe he is as tall as Adrian. They looked as pure and golden as the Sahara Desert. They seem to be searching for something, an innocent soul to take, most likely. Either way, the beauty of them is a memory I will happily hold on to. "What about you Dorian? Would you like to come? I would really appreciate it." My voice shook a little, and I cleared my throat. For some strange reason, I feel like I need him to be there.

"Why not sounds like a good reason to get all dressed up, plus any place where you are is a good place to be." He said the last part softly and for my ears only. Adding, "I would love nothing more than to come for you." My breath caught, and I got a chill on the back of my neck.

My date with Adrian was a few hours away, so Dahlia insisted that we go shopping. Apparently, nothing I own is date appropriate. The only dress I own was the one I wore to my sister's dog's funeral. We went to the mall; Dahlia was annoyingly excited. I can't stop thinking about her brother. What is wrong with me? I have a date with Adrian tonight. Yet I can't shake Dorian from my head. It's almost as if he climbed into my mind and set up camp. Dorian may have the matches, but he is not the one I want to light my fire. I don't need any new burns.

"This is cute. Try it on." Dahlia walked towards me holding a blue dress with a black high waist belt attached. I went into the dressing room and tried it on.

"How does it look?" she asked from the other side of the changing room door.

"It's good, I guess." I told her although I felt like this dress belonged on a street corner somewhere instead of on my body.

"Come out and let me see you." She said.

"I think you should come in here." I replied, as I unlocked the door.

She walked in and looked stunned. "Wow Spyce you look amazing, Adrian is going to die." Dahlia declared.

"Can you find me something else, please?" I asked her.

"You don't like it? The way it's hugging your body, it seems to love you." She said, bringing a light blush to my cheeks.

"I just think it's a little too inviting for a first date, you know?" I answered.

"You know what you are absolutely right, but you should buy it for the future, you know, for when you're ready to give out that invitation?" She teased. She was giggling as she walked out of the dressing room.

After buying a few outfits, matching shoes and accessories, we made our way back home. Dahlia convinced me to allow her to do my hair. She insisted, since she already did my makeup. Apparently, I will feel better when I see the complete picture. She was wrong. I was looking in the mirror at a girl that I didn't recognize. She has thick black curls hanging down her back, wearing a silk black dress trimmed with light gray lace around the bust, her golden-brown skin beaming. She stared back at me with pale gray eyes. She looks beautiful.

"Are you okay, Spyce?" I can hear the concern in Dahlia's voice.

"I'm just overwhelmed." I reassure her.

She walked up to the side of the mirror and spoke. "Adrian isn't the real prize. You are. Remember, He needs to prove to you he's worth your time. Not the other way around."

I turned and looked at her. "Thank you, Dahlia." I said as I turned my back to the stranger in the mirror. I've never felt so awkward before. How I appear on the outside is not how I feel on the inside. I don't feel insecure, I just feel bizarre. I walked out of my room to the kitchen. I need a glass of water; I would hate to pass out on my date.

"Wow" Dorian walked in from the hallway. Stopping in front of the breakfast bar. "I hope you're driving; I don't want you to get stranded when your date passes out." His eyes roved over my body demurely.

"Thanks." I said before I turned towards the fridge, trying to avoid eye contact. I would hate for him to catch me blushing. "I wasn't sure if this look fit my personality." I grabbed a bottle of water.

"You could wear a trash bag and look gorgeous." Dorian said from behind me. I turned around and found myself face to face with him. Why did he have to smell so amazing? It was like springtime mixed with waterfalls.

"You smell wonderful. Is that vanilla?" Dorian whispered. His proximity caught me off guard.

"N-n-no it's brown sugar and hazelnut body cream." I stammered,

"Well, it smells delicious," Dorian growled. I involuntarily shuddered. The sudden knock at the door broke me out of his all-consuming spell and I couldn't have been more grateful.

"I'll get it!" Dahlia shouted as she shuffled off towards the door. I walked into the living room and there he was, my living Adonis.

"Hello Shontelle, you look breathtaking." Adrian's eyes roamed casually over my body.

"Thanks, so do you." I turned to the breakfast bar and grabbed my clutch. Catching a quick glance at Dorian with an unexpected look of annoyance on his face as he looked at Adrian. I tried to ignore it and just walked out the door. Once we were outside, I noted that Adrian walked slightly ahead of me the whole time searching the open space for what I don't know. He never once tried to make small talk, but the silence wasn't uncomfortable. Which was fine, since he wasn't throwing me a bunch of pickup lines. I still felt somewhat awkward and out of place.

He opened the passenger door and closed it gently once I was inside. His car was extremely extravagant. I don't know much about cars, but I knew for a fact that this was an Aston Martin, mainly because Ignatios also has one similar to this one. This car craved attention. Which makes me wonder about the owner. The ride was quiet and inanimate. I wanted to lie back in my seat and go straight to sleep. Adrian broke through the silence.

"Here we are." Adrian announced. I looked out the window

and saw a beautiful building. It stood out amongst all the others. It's pale blue and white coloring standing out amongst the bleak glass uniformity of the other water front properties. It resembles a refurbished plantation, no, not a plantation, the Pantheon in Italy. As Adrian escorted me inside, I noted the beautiful waterfall fountains and lilac lilies, which are my favorite flower. There was a wall with a life like mural of Neptune watching over the ocean during a divine sunset.

We walked slowly through the foyer; I was enjoying the alluring artistry. Adrian halted as he approached the Host's desk. "Buona serata, reservation for two." He said to the host.

"Ciao, signore, so good to see you. Vista Mare isn't the same when you're away." the host exclaimed.

"Estacio, this is Shontelle." Estacio looked at me, jarred. "Ciao Bellissimo, you are divine."

I smiled at Estacio, "Grazie, Signore." He escorted us to a private booth beside an aquarium wall. You could see the Pacific Ocean on the other side of the glass. The view was breath-taking. "So, I take it you come here often?" I asked casually.

"I guess you can say that. I'm one of the owners." He sleekly replied.

"Impressive. I thought Brandon was the only restaurateur I knew." I joked. Adrian gave a small smirk as he watched me from across the table. His green eyes seem to gleam. He is so gorgeous it's gripping. All I could do was stare at him and wonder what made him ask me out. If he has known me for most of my life, why wait until now? I know I haven't been that social, yet still I have no recollection of him since I left middle school. He just abruptly disappeared one day. "Adrian, I'm curious. What made you ask me out today?" He looked down at his hands for a moment before looking up at me with a thoughtful smile. Perhaps it's me, but it felt like he was trying to think about it a little too long for such a simple question.

"I figured after running in to you twice in one day, maybe

fate was on my side. I didn't know if this was my only chance, so I took it."

I observed him carefully. "Thanks for taking that chance, although I was more so referring to why you never asked me out when we were younger. Then one day you just vanished."

"You intimidated me. I had never met anyone that was as exquisite and intelligent as you in my life. Even to this day. I guess the fact that you seemed blind to everything around you helped to increase my restraint. As for my disappearing act, you can thank my mom for that. Her career required us to relocate, and I had to transfer schools my junior year."

"I don't understand." I stated.

"You were so smart and secluded. You spent all of your time consumed with reading or in extracurricular activities. You had gymnastics, dance, debate club, Italian, vocal training, math club, sci-."

I interjected, "Okay, I get it. So, If I would have taken a second to take a breath you might have asked sooner?"

"There is a strong possibility that I still would have been intimidated by your beauty." He said with a chuckle. My face got warm. I could tell I was beaming like a stoplight.

"The food was amazing. I think I have found my new favorite restaurant. Brandon wouldn't mind not losing inventory over me anymore." I jested.

After our meal, we took a stroll outside. We talked more about what we have been up to for the past few years. Although he was rather elusive about the years after he moved away with his mom.

There was a large fountain designed like the Baroque Fountains of Rome. They illuminated the water with blue LED lights. It was breathtaking. As I admired the astonishing beauty of the fountains, I could feel Adrian standing close behind me. I turned around and looked into his beautiful lawn green orbs. He looked back into my eyes and said, "You really don't know how amazing you are, do you?"

I looked up at him curiously, and then he quickly kissed me. I don't know if it was shock or adrenaline, but a sudden bright flash of light that caused me to break the kiss and take a few steps back blinded me. It felt as if my brain erupted and every thought I have ever had rushed to the forefront of my mind. Once my eyes could see clearly, I took another disoriented step back and yelped as I slipped on the wet marble and fell back. Adrian reached out to me only to catch air, then suddenly everything went dark.

I can not believe I was thwarted by a strange spotlight and now because of the erratic pain in my head. I looked up to see Adrian looking down at me with worry and something else in his eyes.

"What happened?" I asked as Adrian helped me up out of the fountain. I wish everything would stop spinning.

"You stepped back and toppled into the fountain. I believe you may have hit your head on the marble." Adrian explained.

"How long was I out?" I asked, still a little dazed.

"Just a few seconds. I think it might be a good idea to get you to a hospital. That's quite a bump on the back of your head." He said in an uneasy tone.

"I'm sure I'm fine. You should probably just take me home, so I can put some ice on it." I replied calmly.

"Are you sure?" he asked skeptically.

"Yes, let's not make it into some big deal." I replied.

"Okay, you sit here. I'll go get the car." Adrian hastened to the parking lot. Once Adrian helped me into the car, I wanted to slap myself. I should have let him take me to the hospital. It would have prolonged our time together. Once we were back at my condo, I was halfway sleepwalking. I was barely aware of my surroundings. Adrian has his arm firmly wrapped around my torso, allowing me to lean into him and use his strength. As we exited out of the elevator,

Adrian decided it would be best for him to carry me the rest of the way.

"You know, if it was that bad of a kiss, you could have just stopped it. You didn't have to run away."Adrian teased as I nestled my head against his chest as he carried me cradled in his strong, capable arms.

"I wasn't trying to run from you. It was that blinding spotlight." I announced.

He looked at me, puzzled. "There wasn't any spotlight. Just the fountain and pathway lights." Adrian told me as he knocked on my condo's door twice.

Dorian opened the door before I could respond. "What the hell happened to her?" He asked Adrian, fury in his eyes and malice in his voice. What the hell is wrong with him? Why is he so upset?

"She fell into a marble pond and hit her head." Adrian answered, ignoring the obvious accusation in Dorian's voice.

"I'll get you some ice for your head." Dorian said to me, losing all the aggression replacing it with gentle concern. He made his way into the kitchen.

"I'm sorry I'm such a klutz." I told Adrian as he laid me down on the living room sofa.

"Don't worry about it. You can make up for it on our next date." Adrian informed me.

"So, there will be another date?" I queried.

"Of course, maybe next time we will go bike riding in the park so that you will already have on a helmet, at least." He teased. I laughed, then groaned from the pain it caused. Dorian returned with a bag of ice wrapped in a hand towel. He also had a glass of water and a bottle of aspirin.

"Thank you," I said b to him with a grateful smile.

"Of course, if you need anything, just let me know." He told me before sitting on the love seat against the other wall.

"I enjoyed tonight; I will call you tomorrow to check in on you."
Adrian placed a tender kiss on my cheek before rising to leave.

"I'll talk to you then. Good night Adrian."

"Good night Shontelle." He walked out the door. I got up a few
minutes later to lock the door and fell onto the coffee table.

Dorian ran over to me. "What happened? Are you okay?" he
asked, on the brink of panic.

"I'm still a little dizz…" My words cut off and once again
everything went dark.

"Well, all of her test results look good. Her CT-Scan shows no
internal bleeding or fractures. She has a mild concussion, there's
no swelling so, she should be fine with plenty of rest. I'm going to
prescribe her something for the pain. Then I'll have her discharge
paperwork." I can hear Doctor Douglas explaining to Brandon.

"When did you get here?" I asked Brandon when we were alone.

"About twenty minutes ago, you were asleep." He replied.

"How did you know I was here? In fact, how did I get here?" I
asked. Everything is still hazy.

"Dahlia's brother brought you here. Adrian had told me what
happened on your date, Klutzo. So, I went to check on you. Dahlia
told me that her brother had brought you here, so we came straight
here." He had an odd expression on his face. I couldn't exactly figure
out what it was.

"So, can I leave now?" I asked.

"We're just waiting for your prescription and discharge papers."
He replied. Dahlia wasn't allowed inside my room because we aren't
related and yet she stayed in the lobby waiting room. If I needed
true evidence, she really was my best friend. It is currently being
presented.

Brandon took me and Dahlia home. After a lecture and a few

teasing jokes, he promised not to say anything to our mom. I noticed an amorous glance exchange between Brandon and Dahlia. Before I turned away to enter my place, Dorian is sitting on the chaise in front of the coffee table with his head in his hands. He looks stressed. I walked over to him and he looked up at me with those golden honey eyes burning through me.

"Thank you for everything."

His response was quite nonchalant and teasing. "Don't worry about it. Just do me a favor and the next time you want to end a date early, just call me and I'll pick you up. You don't have to almost kill yourself to escape."

I gave a small smile and walked to my room but before I went inside Dorian stopped me and smiled, then said softly "Don't worry, I'll keep my eyes on you." He chuckled and then corrected himself. "I mean, I'll keep an eye out for you." I gave him a demurely appreciative look and then continued into my bedroom for some much-needed rest.

When I awoke the next morning, it was to a cool chill running up my spine. My dreams last night were all over the place. It was as if I was watching a clash of movie trailers mashed together that made absolutely no sense. Romantic action packed horror show. The weird thing was the main character was me. Although I wasn't me, I was Dorian in the reflections I came across.

Standing in the center of what appears to be a hotel suite or penthouse, surrounded by attractive women with a look of pure lust beaming from their eyes. They stood perfectly still, as if waiting for something or someone to make a move. After a low whistle coming from Dorian, the women immediately stripped down to their undergarments. Those who have some on. The others simply stood in the nude. Dorian takes three steps backwards and then claps twice and the women instantly start dancing sensually and seductively. After another whistle, the women began dancing erotically with each other. I or Dorian rather was standing against a wall, looking over what was happening before him.

"It would please me if you all made each other come." Dorian's voice had a strange yet alluring tone. The women, at that instance, pleasured each other slowly at first. It became feverish and chaotic as some fought over each other to do what has been requested. Eventually every woman connected to a pussy by their mouth in a perfectly linked daisy chain. The

moans echoed throughout the open space. Cries of pleasure and writhing bodies made the floor look like waves of ecstasy.

"I would love to know who you all work for and why you are really here." Dorian said in that strange tone. The women all spoke simultaneously. Dorian interrupted, very calm but firm.

"One at a time. You first." he pointed to a curvy, dark-skinned woman with straight black hair that was cut into a Bob.

"We all work for an escort service. Our boss, Nina Petrova, sent us to you for your pleasure." her eyes were glossy and hooded.

"Is that the only reason you are here, I would love to know?" Dorian Asked, with his alluring voice.

"It also meant for us to distract you for a while." a brunette with pale skin and a slim frame responded.

"Ladies, it would make me so happy if you all got dressed and went home and stayed there until Monday, no matter what anyone else tells you to do." The women all dressed and left quietly. The dream then jumped to a bar fight where two men brutally fought each other. Once they were too bloody and battered to continue, Dorian's voice says to them both, "now, go do that to your boss and I will be sincerely pleased."

The dream only got more bloody and violent, as if Dorian was James Bond with the power to compel anyone in his path. The man is gorgeous, but it's as if his voice held some control over people that made them want to do his bidding.

I tried to push the dream away, thinking so much about my new sexy as sin roommate can not be good for me.

"*Dahlia, why* do we have to go shopping every time we're invited somewhere?" I asked quasi annoyed.

"We don't have to but, you have nothing to wear to your mother's party. Plus, you desperately needed to get out of the house." She replied.

"I'm fine, okay? What happened on Monday is over and, in the past, now. So, let's just leave it there, along with Adrian. I blew it and now he knows I really am a weirdo. I am sure he has moved on." I adamantly told her.

"I highly doubt that he has moved on. I'm pretty sure that is all in your head." Dahlia assured me.

"If it's all in my head, how come he hasn't dropped by, called or even sent a text?" I asked.

"Maybe he's been busy. You said that he's refurbishing his place and not to mention he still has work to do and he is working on his thesis. Graduation is only a few months away. You're the only genius here. The rest of us have to try really hard for our first PhD, and you're on your second and third." Dahlia responded.

I must admit, she was inadvertently convincing me. It is possible that Adrian hasn't been avoiding me for the past week. Perhaps he has just been consumed with work or the construction of his home. We left the boutique empty handed. Dahlia suggested we order take out and watch movies. Unfortunately, that would have to wait. I received a call from Doctor Douglas for a follow-up appointment this afternoon. I dropped Dahlia off at home and told her I would meet up with her after. On my way to Dr. Douglas' office, I replayed Monday night over in my head. I just don't understand what happened. What was that blinding light that caused me to step back? I walked in to the doctor's office and the nurse told me to wait in the back office. Dr. Douglas has been my doctor since I was born. I used to joke around and say he left pediatrics just so that he could stay my doctor.

"I apologize for the wait, Shontelle. I have looked at your lab work and your CT scan again. Everything appears to be normal. There is some fluctuation in your temporal lobe. It doesn't show any damage. In fact, it looks to be the strongest part of your brain as of now. It is common for the temporal lobe to fluctuate more in people with Eidetic memory. Your mind is giving you extra storage space, which means your temporal lobe is expanding certain neurons to different parts of your brain. This has been a theory of the possibility of developing psychokinesis telepathy." He explained.

"Dr. Douglas, are you trying to tell me I am some type of psychic? I asked, dumfounded.

"It is only a theory. Further testing would be necessary to know for sure. Have you talked to your mom about what happened?" He replied.

I grabbed my things. "No, not yet. I'm sorry Doc, but I need to go."

I left the clinic immediately. I don't know how, but I'm pretty sure that Dr. Douglas Is losing his marbles. How could he believe such ridiculousness? I think he should probably get a CT scan for himself and then prepare for his retirement. I'm guessing he will contact my mom about this, so I have that chaos to look forward to. When I got home, I didn't tell Dahlia what the good doctor said. I suggested we stay in and make it a movie night. She was all for it.

Of course, her movie choices were the total opposite of mine. Dahlia enjoys horror movies that are gruesome and disgusting. I don't watch horror films because of the amount of blood and carnage. The black and white classics are more my speed. After all, they're more comedic than frightening. Not to mention I don't want the permanent image of a decapitation etched into my memory. Before she could start the first movie, I asked her if I could make a movie selection. She sat in her seat and grabbed a slice of pizza. I put on a movie she would love about a thrilling romance that would normally be forbidden. Between a young high school girl and a soulless vampire. After the first movie, I wanted to go out for dessert.

"Hey, Where's Dorian?" I asked.

"Why?" Dahlia asked suspiciously.

"I was just thinking that we should go to The Lost Pattern for dessert. I am seriously craving Brandon's Tiramisu. It would only be polite to ask him to join us if he is here." I casually replied.

"You're right, it would be polite." She agreed. She went into the guest room. I put the leftovers away. Dahlia returned shortly after I finished loading the dishwasher. She appeared to be perplexed.

"What's wrong? Is everything all right?" I asked, concerned.

"Of course Dorian doesn't want to go. He claims to be very exhausted." She said to me with just enough doubt to let me know she was not sure if he was being truthful.

"I'm sorry to hear that. We can bring him something back. I'm sure he's ok. After all, didn't you once call him the king of the night? I'm sure he just finally gave in to his body to get some much-needed rest." I told her as we walked out of the door. She agreed.

"So, you did end things with Vanessa?" I asked Brandon, who looks particularly content for someone going thru a serious break-up after an eight-year relationship. Brandon and Vanessa have been together since they were in high school.

"It was time for us to go our separate ways. I still care about her. I just don't see us having a future. We've grown apart." Brandon said, not even the slightest bit somber. He seemed more-so relieved than anything.

"I hope you both find someone that not only makes you happy but also makes you complete." I told him.

Dahlia and I arrived at the Lost Pattern twenty minutes ago. When we walked In, we saw Vanessa, Brandon's now ex-girlfriend, highly intoxicated and very disturbed. When I asked her how she was, she looked at me with all the fire burning within her and aforementioned, that I should ask my brother. Something that I wish I could retract. You would think that his story would sound depressing or filled with anger, but it was very buoyant and enthusiastic. I haven't taken anytime to really get to know Vanessa on a personal level. She seemed sweet and respectful. I personally don't understand why Brandon decided to break things off with her now. Well, I'm sure he did what he thought was best for them both.

"I came by to get some of your famous Tiramisu." I announced.

"We're all out for the night, but I have some cannolis or a chocolate and raspberry torte." Brandon told Dahlia and I.

"We will take some of both. Can you make it enough for three? Her brother may want some as well." I requested.

"Six desserts coming right up. I'll be back in a few minutes." Brandon made his way to the kitchen. Dahlia and I sat in a booth and watched the crowd at the bar. A few guys from the only fraternity on campus were celebrating a birthday. Extreme public intoxication, fun.

"Don't turn around!" Dahlia blurted out, causing me to freeze and tense up.

"Why not? What happened?" I asked, befuddled.

"It's Adrian, and he's not alone. He has an attractive piece of arm candy with him." Dahlia stated.

Suddenly my heart dropped, and I felt hollow inside. So, all my assumptions were accurate: he has moved on to the next girl. She's probably not some clumsy idiot. That's why he has been avoiding me, to save me from ridicule and humiliation. He chose an alternate approach compared to Brandon's blunt conversation. Adrian decided to just ghost me all together and just move on with someone new. I casually glanced over my shoulder and the back of the booth that was a few inches to high for me to see over, which forced me to stretch up; Adrian was walking in our direction with a beautiful blonde woman. She had a very slim figure with all the right number of curves in all the right places. She had to be a model or an Amazon from Themyscira. I turned around and laid my head on the table.

"Hey Dee, how's it going?" Adrian asked Dahlia.

"Oh, you know, just waiting for Brandon to bring out dessert." Dahlia uttered nervously.

"Do you mind if we sit with you? There aren't any tables available?" Adrian asked.

"I don't think that would be a good idea." Dahlia said with dismay.

Adrian was on the side of me but behind the booth's partition when he asked. "Are you on a date?"

Before Dahlia replied, I stood up and blurted out, "No, she's just trying to be a good and protective friend. But unfortunately, the humiliation is still strong. I'll save myself from further embarrassment and leave." I turned to Dahlia and asked. "Can you just grab the dessert and meet me at home?" she nodded her head in agreement. I walked with haste out the front door.

I heard Adrian behind me shouting, "Shontelle, wait, don't leave. I need to talk to you."

I turned around as he caught up to me outside. "What do you want from me? Was that not humiliating enough for you? I get it you're not interested; you've moved on to someone better." I announced, annoyed and frustrated.

"What are you talking about? I am beyond interested in you." Adrian declared to me.

"I find that hard to believe, since I haven't seen or heard from you in almost two weeks. Then to make things worst I run into you here with that beautiful European model on your arm." I told him.

"Okay, first, I have been busy with my home renovations, so I haven't been able to come and see you. Second, I called you a few times with no answer or response to any of my texts. And finally, that so called European model is my baby sister Cassandra." By the time Adrian was at the end of his explanation, I was so ashamed of my behavior I couldn't even respond coherently.

"I would like to apologize for that…. That… I don't know what that was." I wanted to run as far away as fast as possible. I wish I were the flash and could run back in time before this conversation ever happened. "Wait, you said you called and texted me? I never got either." I said as I reached into my pocket to grab my phone. Adrian pulled out his phone as well. He showed me the text that he sent. "I see the problem; the number is wrong that five should be a three." We both laughed. I felt so ridiculous.

"Does this mean I'll get another chance?" He asked.

"Yes." I replied immediately. "Would you like to escort me to the party tomorrow night?"

Adrian's smile makes my heart flutter like a hummingbird's wings. "That sounds great. Would you mind if I also brought my sister with us? She doesn't have any friends here, and she hasn't been out since she's been back from Europe?" he asked.

"Of course, maybe I'll just meet you guys there. I am supposed to be going with Dahlia and Dorian." I responded.

"That would be ok with me as long as you save me a dance." He said.

"That I can promise you." I confirmed.

Adrian placed both of his hands on my cheeks, gently cupping my face as he pressed his lips to mine, coaxing them open with his tongue. His lips are soft and his tongue tastes like strawberries. He lifted his head. "Now that we are both on the same page, would you like to join me back inside so that I can introduce you to my sister?"

I could feel the blood rushing to my face. I don't want to go back inside and face everyone after my embarrassing episode. I also don't want him to stop kissing me. Just before I could answer, Dahlia walked outside with two to-go boxes in hand, saving me from an awkward situation. "Hey you're still here. I thought you had left." She seemed troubled by something.

"I was just leaving, but I really didn't want to take an Uber." I told her. After I rushed out, so hastily I hadn't even realized I rode here with Dahlia.

"Are you ready now, or do you need a moment?" Dahlia asked.

"I'm ready." I turned my attention back to Adrian. "I'll see you tomorrow night." I said, as Dahlia and I retreated. Adrian gave me that beautiful soul marking smile as he nodded his confirmation.

"So, are you going to tell me what happened, or are you waiting for me to question you?" Dahlia asked me as soon as we settled in her car.

"Let's just get out of here and I'll fill you in on the way home." I replied, not looking forward to the conversation of my idiocy.

Once we were home, Dahlia was still laughing. She apologized to me. Since it was her assumption, that caused me to draw the wrong conclusion. To make things worst, she knew Adrian had a younger sister, but she hasn't seen her in a few years so she didn't recognize her with one hell of a glow up.

"Dorian isn't here, so you won't have to hear me tell him your sad tale of misapprehension." She giggled.

"That's great Dahlia. I'm going to bed. I'll see you in the morning." I told her, exhausted but elated. I can almost guarantee Adrian, and that kiss will premiere in my dreams tonight.

What is that sound? I look over at the clock on my nightstand. It's three o'clock in the morning. Is someone trying to break in? I quickly get out of my bed to go investigate. The sounds are coming from the living room. I stopped in front of the coffee table and picked up a small marble statue of Athena, an unwanted gift from the most annoying stepfather ever. I slowly turned and the front door opened too quickly. It slammed into the wall. A young female who appeared to be of Spanish heritage slowly stumbled in. "Hey sexy! where should I drop my curves?" she asked, the air behind her.

"The first room to the left when you enter the hallway." The air replied in a bored but sultry voice I could pick out in the middle of a rave. The drunk girl swayed her way towards the guest room, all the while trying to stay upright. Dorian slowly entered the condo with his shoulders slouched, head down and face void of any emotion. He looked up at me with golden orbs that look trapped in a hollow void and said, "I apologize for the noisy bimbo. She's had a few."

"No problem, I was just getting something to drink." I lied.

"Oh really? Was Athena helping you?" He asked sarcastically.

I sat the statue down on the end table and headed back towards my room. "You forgot your drink." I heard him say just before I slammed my room door shut. I went over and plopped on to my bed and shoved my body under the comforter. I tried to force myself into unconsciousness. I wanted to make sure that I was completely unconscious when they made things go bump in the night.

When I woke the next morning, I had yet another headache. They have been consistent ever since my date with Adrian. They aren't as strong as when I hit my head. That was more like having a jackhammer go all in on my Occipital lobe. Now it's just a lot of pressure. It feels like a bear is giving my brain a hug. I dragged myself out of bed and walked to the restroom in the hallway, instead of the one in my room, knowing that I will find a big bottle of aspirin in the medicine cabinet. Once I was inside of the restroom, I turned on the faucet to splash some water on my face to help me wake up and I immediately hear a loud curse and a sound of pain come from the shower. It's Dorian's voice, knowing that I immediately turned the water off and left the restroom before he saw me and assumed his cause for discomfort was intentional. Although it wasn't, my obvious pleasure in his discomfort would suggest otherwise.

I made my way to the kitchen. I grabbed two eggs, cheese, pre-cut peppers, spinach and some bacon. I deserve a nice omelet. I grabbed a nonstick pan and placed it on the stovetop.

"Good morning sweetheart, did you and Athena sleep well?" Dorian asked, with a dark sarcastic tone of his humor. He looks like he has been up all night.

"Do you ever dry off in the actual bathroom?" His body was dripping wet. I clenched my thighs together because he wasn't the only one. He is glistening.

"Usually, I'm not forced out of the shower because of childish pranks?" Dorian announced, his voice agitated and the accusation clear. "Anyhow, I know that jealousy can cause some people to act out of character." He continued.

"Are you insinuating that I've done something to you out of jealousy?" I asked defensively.

"I saw you leave out of the restroom." He said with a smug grin.

Then added, "If you wanted to see me naked so bad, you could have just asked me. I'm more than willing to oblige."

I stood there, astonished by the direction this conversation has gone. I abruptly realized that he was still, in fact, naked, wearing nothing but a bath towel. Somewhere in our conversation, he slowly made his way into the kitchen with me. He was close enough for me to feel the steam rising from his body. "Tell me, Spyce what is it you were hoping to see?" He asked, his voice filled with pure seduction.

"It was an accident. I wasn't paying attention, and I forgot you were here. I assumed it was Dahlia that was in the shower." I explained, exasperated by his body's proximity to mine.

"Is that so?" He slowly leaned in towards me. I closed my eyes and held my breath. Suddenly the loud piercing fire alarm went off, jerking my attention away from this male siren. I look over at my omelet, that is now burned into the pan. I quickly turn off the fire and dropped the pan into the sink, turning on the spout. Dahlia runs into the living room in a full panic. Dorian tells her it was a false alarm. He added that I'm not much of a chef like my brother. The guest room door opens unexpectantly and the girl from last night appears panicked and only wearing a long T-shirt. Which could only belong to Dorian. I completely forgot she was here. Evidently so did Dorian. He walked over to her and tells her, "Everything is fine and under control. You can go back to the room. I'll be there in a moment."

"Well hurry, we have plans." She whined to him. Although, I'm the one she's looking at with animosity as she walks back into the guest room.

"I'm sorry about that, she…." I didn't need to hear anything else from him. I was already in my room before he could finish his statement. I locked the door, got showered, and dressed before I texted Dahlia that I would wait for her by her car. I had promised her we could try again for dresses to wear tonight. With Adrian's assurance that he will surely be present, I definitely want to look my best.

"Can you believe my annoying brother had the audacity to bring some random girl to our place? He claims it was because he couldn't allow her to drive herself home drunk. So, he says. What were they out of Ubers last night?" Dahlia was ranting and raving about the girl in Dorian's T-shirt.

I personally have had enough of all things that have to do with Dorian, so I have no problem changing the subject. "I like that gown it makes you look Classy and sexy at the same time." I told her as she swayed back and forth in a cream ballroom gown trimmed with green lace.

"You're right, it looks nice, but I want to wear something less modest and more Va-va-voom," she exclaimed.

I went back into the dressing room to try on the gown she chose for me. I looked at myself in the long slender red gown with the slit down the front that seems to climb higher in my mind. I stepped out to show Dahlia. "Maybe you should wear this and I'll wear that?" I suggested.

She let out a giggle, then said. "I'll take that, but I have something better for you." She handed me another gown. I tried this one on and I had to admit I love everything about it. It is flawless. I have a dress. I didn't show Dahlia. I told her I will show her tonight. We purchased our dresses, and we left the boutique.

I sat in the back seat of the town car that my mother sent for me. She had, of course, assumed that I would be alone. No need to waste money on an SUV or stretch just for me. Fortunately, Dorian planned his own transportation to the party. Dahlia opted to ride with me, knowing my mother was expecting me to be alone. She wanted to give her a pleasant surprise.

"I'll go first. Just follow behind me and ignore the cameras. You look drop dead gorgeous." Dahlia told me as she opened the car door. I got out of the car behind Dahlia immediately. I didn't want to linger and bring more attention to myself. I gave my shawl to Bernard, our home manager.

"Hello Miss Spyce, Welcome home."

"Hello Bernie, it's so nice to see you." I replied. Bernard has worked for my grandmother, Charlotte, also known as Nona Charlie, since she was in her late twenties. They had some problems that caused them to reconsider his employment when my grandmother married my grandfather Saul.

Of course, I know why. They were intimate friends until Bernard asked Nona Charlie to marry him. What would her rich parents think about her marrying a house servant so he stayed with her until she couldn't stand it anymore by that time my mom was of age and married herself and she couldn't bear to see him go, so she had him work for her. At 72 years old, Bernie is a family heirloom.

I walked towards the main hall of my mother's estate where I saw her standing at the top of the staircase all dolled up in a black floor length A-line, V-neck chiffon dress. She has her hair pinned back with loose curls that shaped her face. From a distance, I could have mistaken her for my older sister if it were not for the paleness of her skin. She stands next to Ignatius as they welcome the incoming guests. "Shontelle, my dear, you look amazing. I always knew you would eventually get your fashion genes working." She said, delighted by my appearance. My gown is a fitted satin and lace masterpiece, a lush purple with black lace trim. It clings to my body like a second skin, backless with a v-neck line.

"Well, I can't take credit for my appearance. My friend Dahlia picked this dress out for me and helped with my hair." I told her as I turned to introduce Dahlia as she was stepping up behind me.

"Hello Mrs. Spyce, it's a pleasure to meet you." Dahlia politely said.

"It's a pleasure to meet you Dahlia and please call me Janine." my mom tells her, trying to be casual. She kept my dad's last name and never changed it to Drakos.

"Of course." Dahlia replied.

We walked down to the dining Hall where a buffet of the finest cuisine has been laid out. Of course, to keep my brother involved in this party, my mom had his restaurant do the catering, which means he will have to show up to check on his crew. Yes, my mom is tricky like that. She can be quite the puppeteer. One year in middle school she had me convinced if I didn't wear skirts and dress shoes I would get kicked out of school for an indecent wardrobe. I discovered the truth from other slackers; I stopped believing what she said about how I dressed.

My sister Julissa was making herself a plate when we approached the table.

"Hello Jewels." I turned to Dahlia. "I'd like for you to meet my friend Dahlia."

Julissa looked at me like I just gave her news of an asteroid plummeting towards earth. "Hello, it's nice to meet you. You are the first of Shonnie's friends I've met. I haven't had this pleasure. Everyone is due a miracle at some point." She said before she staggered drunkenly towards her table. She almost made it until another guest walked into her. Causing her plate to smash into her gown. Julissa let out a loud screech as she pushed the guy out of the way, then ran off to the powder room. The guy that ran into her coincidently was Adrian.

Julissa is the eldest of the three of us. It would be hard to believe based on her immature and reckless nature. She's like the classic stereotypical heiress self centered, fake, fame whore. Her biggest issue is being the least interesting person. Not to mention her serious daddy issues. So, of course, she's our stepfather's favorite.

Adrian sees me and walks over to me and Dahlia. "Hey Dee. Hello Shontelle" he was still looking directly at me when he said. "You guys look fantastic," he smiled and my breath hitched at the brilliance of it.

"Thanks. You look very dashing yourself." Dahlia told him.

I smiled and nodded in agreement. He's dressed in a well-tailored black tuxedo with a green shirt under his jacket that brought out his eyes like shining jade. He had a James Bond kind of aura to him. "Where is Cassandra?" I asked.

"She's freshening up in the restroom." Adrian replied. "Would you like to join me for a dance, of course, if that's OK with Dee?"

"That's absolutely fine by me." Dahlia says, giving me the 'get it girl,' eyes.

"I'll come find you later." I told her.

Adrian reaches for me to join him on the dance floor. I place my hand in his and he leads me to the edge of the dance floor. After gently sliding my hair off my shoulder, he turned my back into his front and placed his hands on my hips as he rocked our bodies slowly from side to side. The song playing was slow and sensually seductive. I swayed my hips as I leaned into him completely. His hands traced up my arms. His touch caused me to shiver. His warm breath against my neck sent a wave of heat straight to my core. I turned around, wrapped my arms around his neck, and pressed my body into his. Adrian wrapped his arms around my waist and pressed his lips gently to the base of my neck. "I haven't been able to stop thinking about you. Having you in my arms right now feels like a dream come to reality."

I shivered at his words. His heady scent of pinewood and citrus has my mind reeling. We continued to sway back and forth, our bodies tightly fitted together. I ran my palms down his shoulders to his biceps. My hands seem tinier than usual against his bulging muscles. I couldn't resist giving them a small squeeze. Adrian's hands slowly descended from my waist to my full hips, where his fingers slowly glided, making small circles against my skin. Taking complete advantage of the completely backless gown. He seems to enjoy the touch of my skin. He pulled me in closer, crushing my chest to his.

He whispered into my ear. "Let's go out to the Veranda for a moment?" I nodded and let him lead the way to my mother's private garden.

Once I walked out towards my mother's alluring oasis, it reminded me of our first date. "You know, I'm not sure it's safe for me to be in the garden with you. Remember what happened last time, because I'll never forget?"

Adrian stopped and turned to face me. "Well, maybe we can try to replace that memory with a better one and also avoid all fountains." he grinned playfully.

"It wouldn't hurt to try." I agreed.

He pressed his lips softly to mine, and I instantly daydreamed. I can see Adrian getting ready for the party. He is standing in front of a full-length mirror trying to tie his bow tie. There is also someone else present, a beautiful slender woman standing in the reflection behind him, wearing a red satin dress with a plunging neckline. She has blonde hair pulled back in an elegant bun.

"Shontelle, did you hear me?" Adrian was asking, looking down at me. "I'm sorry. What were you saying?" I asked, confused and trying to understand when he stopped kissing me.

"I said Cassandra is looking for me inside. Would you like to meet her officially?" Adrian asked, already escorting me back inside.

"Of course, that would be nice. I'm afraid her opinion of me may have been tainted because of our first encounter." I replied as we made our way back inside to the party.

When I spotted Cassandra, a wall of confusion instantly hit me. Standing before me was an open view of Déjà vu. She was wearing a red satin dress with a plunging neckline. Her blonde hair is styled in a tight, neat ballerina's bun. She is talking to Dorian, whom is wearing black tailored slacks, a black dress shirt and a dark wine tuxedo jacket. He looks amazing.

"Cassandra, can you join me for a moment?" Adrian asked as he was already pulling her away. "There's someone I would like for you to meet. This is Shontelle Spyce."

"Oh, hello, so you're the cultivating woman that my brother is obsessed with." she announced. I could feel the heat of the blood rushing to my face. "now, I understand why." she added teasingly.

"You look beautiful as well, just like a classic movie star." I replied.

Adrian was looking behind his sister at Dorian. "Cassie, what was he talking to you about?" Adrian asked Cassandra.

"Not much. He was just complimenting my dress." She said with excitement in her voice.

"You should know better than that. You already know about his reputation." Adrian said.

"So. Didn't I also have a so called bad rep once too? You know

I don't feed into the speculation and commentary of others." Cassandra replied vehemently.

"What about on an international scale?" Adrian countered.

His sister looked over at Dorian, then back at Adrian, and said, "I still don't care. He has never shown me anything more than pure kindness?"

Adrian looked at me, then asked, "Could you give us a moment? I will be right back?" Adrian said as he pulled Cassandra to the side.

"Apparently your boyfriend wants to keep all the Beautiful Creatures locked away." Dorian said, sneaking up beside me as I watched Adrian lecturing his younger sibling, nearly shocking my soul from my body.

I was so focused on Adrian and Cassandra; I didn't notice his approach. "What the hell, you need to be wearing a warning bell or something. That's his younger sister. He's just making sure she doesn't get herself in any trouble." I declared to him.

I turned to walk away, but he gently grabbed me by my elbow to stop me. "Are you so appalled by me you can't spare me a moment of your time, or are you so consumed by him you can't endure being away from him?"

I turned and looked into his sexy, mesmerizing gold eyes and said, "Yes."

I walked away towards the restroom. A large part of me wanted to stay, to turn around and just stay in his presence and drink him in. I wanted to be utterly consumed by him. I can't fathom why, yes, he's gorgeous, but I seem to have this desperate pull towards him. Like for some unknown reason, we should never be separated. I made my way to the powder room to pull myself together.

11

Once I was positive that I had pulled myself back together, I withdrew myself from the safety of the powder room everyone had gathered in a circle to watch two contortionists perform a daring act. I watched with awe and merriment. I leaned against the wall near a six foot gilded mirror and watched the captivating performers. Once the show ended, the music started up once more.

Everyone piled on the dance floor dancing to the enticing hip hop music. Although I am feeling the music's call, I opted to remain off to the side just bobbed my head along to the beat. Dahlia was grinding against my brother with her hands clasped around his neck. While his hands were on her hips guiding them. To the right of them Dorian and Cassie were dancing less provocatively, although Cassie seemed to have wandering hands that Dorian didn't approve of. Despite his usual flirtation, he was being respectful. I don't think Adrian approves either. The daggers his eyes were shooting are lethal. My first glimpse of anger from him and somehow it makes him look dangerously sexy. Those green eyes are heated like a wildfire. His strong jaw is clenched so tight his teeth have to be made of steel. His fist are balled so tight, his knuckles are white. As the song ends, the dance floor clears once more for another performance. Adrian quickly pulls his sister to the side and they bicker softly. Cassie's face is warped with irritation and embarrassment. She pushes Adrian away, then walks off. Adrian hangs his head in frustration. After a few deep breaths, he brings his head up to lock eyes with me. Instantly finding his composure, Adrian gives me a beautiful smile and then makes his way towards me. "Hey, I'm going to take Cassie home before she does something she regrets. I'll be back though, so save me a dance, okay?"

I nodded, and he rewarded me with a kiss on the cheek that caused my stomach to fill with butterflies. I then continued to watch the performers. They were exceptional. Gravity defying stunts that could put you into a trance. So Captivating I lost all sense of my social anxiety. Once the performers ended their show, I looked for Dahlia, who seemed to have vanished.

"Now why is such a gorgeous being like yourself not out on the dance floor?" Dorian asked softly into my ear, causing me to jump. He had approached me from behind, causing my heart to pound in my ears.

"Seriously, I'm ordering you a collar with a bell tonight. Actually, I am looking for your womb, mate. Have you seen her?" I asked, trying to calm my nerves and catch my breath.

"Last I saw, she was going upstairs with your Big Brother." Dorian stated. "I guess some of the Spyces actually have some heat to them."

I turned to look him in the eyes to tell him he wouldn't be able to last a minute with the inferno that blazes within me. Somehow, I instead became completely overwhelmed by his near presence. It's as if his golden orbs were beckoning me to give him whatever he desired. My instincts wanted me to turn and kiss him with all the fire burning inside my soul. Instead, I looked at him and let the flames of the fire he ignited show in my eyes.

"That's more like it." Dorian observed me with devious eyes, as if he knew exactly what would happen next and he was just waiting patiently for me to confirm it. I turned and rushed away. I bumped into a server and stumbled, landing promptly on my ass. The server reached out immediately and helped me up. The moment my hand was in his, I had a flash of some people looking up at a television screen with a shadowy figure holding a picture of someone. A young woman with midnight black curls and light golden brown skin with a distinct oval birthmark on her neck below her left ear. Wait, what the hell, that woman is me?

"Are you alright? It's a miracle you didn't hit your head." He helped me up quickly.

"Thank you for your help. You're a Knight?" I professed.

"Actually, I'm more of a delivery man." He ominously chuckled. Then he was gone after being called over by a small group of men covered in tattoos and piercings dressed in uniforms different from the other staff.

I walked outside to the Veranda. I need fresh oxygen. My head is spinning. The delivery man came out, offering me a glass of champagne. I accepted the glass and took a big sip, focusing on the bubbles as they move down my throat. "Thanks" I said.

"You don't seem that interested in this party." The delivery man pointed out.

"It's not exactly my thing. I'd prefer to be at home cuddled with a warm blanket, hot chocolate and a good book. I guess champagne will have to suffice." I finished the glass.

He seems sweet. He definitely has a cute roguish charm. Boyish facial features and an average height and build, with some very toned biceps. He couldn't be much older than me, maybe a few years older. "Do you have a name delivery man?" I asked.

"I do, but I don't think now would be a good time for that information. I might share it when my work here is done." If this guy was going for a mysterious stranger vibe, he missed the mark and leaped to just weird.

I swayed slightly. My head is suddenly rushed with a wave of dizziness. "I think I need to sit down. Don't let me hold you up. Complete your delivery." I said, while trying to keep myself steady.

"Actually, I'm here for a pickup. I almost forgot the most important thing." He looks straight into my eyes before saying, "Grab her!"

Four men appeared on the Veranda from each side and I jumped up and instantly regretted it. The world was spinning around me.

"What the hell is going on?" My words are coming out slurred. My hands reach out, holding on to the delivery man standing in front of me.

"You would think women these days would stop accepting random drinks from men. Especially when you don't even know them. Do you even know what you look like?" My body went lax and everything went dark. The last thing I heard was the shatter of glass as my champagne flute hit the ground. My body was lifted just as my mind drifted into complete nothingness.

12

Where are we going? This is driving me insane? I woke up to discover that I was blindfolded and wearing noise canceling headphones. I may not see or hear anything, but my sense of smell can't be concealed. This is bad. We're at the beach, not a sandy beach, but a rocky one somewhere near a lighthouse. I can smell the breeze and despite the annoying blindfold, I can see the light as it comes and goes in a rhythmic pattern. I wish I knew what was happening and why I was being kidnapped. Just who are these people? The question brought in obvious answers: I'm an heiress, my family's fortune is world news. Why would they take me? Yes, I'm a Spyce, but I'm the least publicized one of us all. It shocked most people to learn my family's lineage. I'm not someone that publicly associates with Spyce industries. My brother and sister made it part of their daily endeavors. My brother Brandon used the publicity from our name for his restaurant. I can understand that. My oldest sister Julissa used it for different reasons. Like for status or to gain new friends and a higher social standing. Which she only wants so that she may gain some sense of power and control. Her only true goal in life. I can't believe they did this during my mother's party. I'm glad Adrian left early to take his sister home, where they are safe from harm. The light pattern has stopped and the windy breeze is now gone. We must be at our destination. The guy carrying me suddenly laid me down on what feels like a leather sofa. The smell of sandalwood and hickory fills the air. I must be in a cabin. I could feel the heat of an exposed fire place, its warmth dancing on my skin. I cannot believe this is happening to me. Why is this happening to me? What have I done to deserve this? The blindfold is being removed, along with the noise canceling headphones. My suspicions have been confirmed. I am in a cabin, not your everyday hunter's cabin in the Woods, away from civilization. This was a mansion size luxury retreat kind of cabin. The living area has a full bar taking over the entire wall to my right. The top half of the wall is covered in mirrors that make the room expand out even further.

"Hello Shontelle, I apologize for the aggressive extraction from your mother's home. It was the only way I could assure that I could get you here safely." The voice of benevolence came from a tall, small framed, red-haired woman with bright green eyes that remind me of Peridot. She seems familiar, although I'm positive I've never met her in my life. Maybe we have crossed paths in passing.

"I'm sorry, I'm confused. How is kidnapping me, keeping me safe, and safe from what, exactly?" I asked, completely overwrought.

"Please, have no fear. Everything will be explained to you in due time. First, I must ask, were you harmed or hurt during your transport here?" The familiar stranger asked.

"No, I'm just perfect." I replied, sarcasm dripping from each word. "Now, can you please tell me why I had to be kidnapped, gagged, blindfolded and sound blocked by armed strangers, for my safety, not to mention drugged?" I was angry and irritated beyond my nature, and yet still somehow very intrigued. I would definitely fight for my freedom had this woman not implied what she had.

"Alright then, allow me to introduce myself. My name is Nuala O'Connor. I have no intention of causing you any harm. What happened tonight was merely a preventive extraction to protect you from SILA, an underground worldwide terrorist organization. We were informed of a kidnapping attempt on a possible weapon by these terrorists." Nuala explained.

"What do you mean, weapon? I'm a person, not a missile!" I exclaimed with conviction.

"You are one of a few gifted people. You just haven't had the proper training to develop your gifts. If trained properly, you can be one of the most powerful people to walk on this planet. The possibilities for you with your particular gifts are endless." The Red Queen continued on with her psychotic explaination.

"Oh OK, I get it now. That explains so much. This is obviously a prank dreamed up from my fame whoring sister. Where is she? Come on out Jewels, I'm smarter than this and I know when someone is messing with me." The room is quiet. No one makes a move. Instead, all eyes are on me. Everyone looking at me with pity, like I've gone mad.

"I know this is hard to fathom, but I can show you if you allow it?" Nuala said. Before I could respond, she sat next to me and continued on. "Do you know how far back your memory bank goes? Do you know how to access any of your memories from any point of time?" She queried.

Choosing to humor her and not question how she knows about my eidetic memory. I answer honestly. "Something familiar can trigger some memories bringing it to the surface, but once brought to my attention, I can remember every detail of any event that occurred in my life that I was present for. By not having an accurate conception of time before I was five years old, I can describe events that happened since the first time my mother breastfed me."

Nuala smiled like she found life on mars. "Has your mind ever displayed a memory that seemed displaced? That couldn't possibly belong to you?" she asked.

I could sense that she already knows the answer be I tell her, anyway "I have been having a few random day dreams that feel like real memories but couldn't possibly be mine. I just assumed they were dreams portraying themselves as memories. It can sometimes get complicated, trying to differentiate fact from fiction. I have a very vivid imagination." I conclude.

"You have an insanely powerful mind. My theory is that you have the ability to see into other people's memories, not just yours. Which means you can access their minds." Nuala theorized. She continued on, "Let me tell you a little about your family history. I'm sure you know all about your father's history in medical science. What you may not know is that your father and mother were both elite chemist, who graduated top of their classes. During their last year of medical school, they were both sought by a headhunter from the world's largest government funded pharmaceutical company."

I interrupted her history lesson and pointed out that I know this information.

"Well, what I could guess is that you don't know what form of government funded their research."

"OK, you have my attention." I said.

"They were funded through the CIA and NSA in a joined effort." Nuala said, watching me closely as my eyes nearly popped out of my head.

"Wait, that can't be right. Are you saying my parents are out were spies?" I asked incredulously. "You are off your rocker if that is what you believe."

"No, your parents were not spies. They were both just very talented biochemists that were brought in for medical research. But they showed extreme talent in microbiology and biochemistry. So they became part of a team that specialized in medical reformation against bioterrorism. Within five years, your parents had created serums that could fight off most deadly forms of bacteria. Your father and mother got married in the early years of the team's development. Two years later, your mother had accidentally become exposed to an unknown virus that had yet to be tested. The virus would attack the person's genetic infrastructure, causing mutations and mental fabrications. Your father developed a cure that altered the person's genetic markers randomly so that the virus couldn't sustain or adapt. After two weeks, the virus had left her system, but her genetic infrastructure had become permanently altered. The team disbanded after they discovered they were being manipulated by their employers." Nuala surmised.

"Ok, so what exactly does that have to do with me?" I asked my patience running out for her to get to the point.

She continued, "Your father began an independent pharmaceutical company. Spyce industries are a lot more than just cleaning products and pharmacies. The root of the business' financial wealth is the pharmaceuticals that are developed through labs hidden under shell companies. Your father's legacy that is now run by your mother."

I couldn't keep a straight face. The wonder and curiosity had to be planted on my face. "Has she ever mentioned what happened to your father? If you don't know, maybe you should ask her next time you see her." Nuala advised.

"Nice to know that I'll have the opportunity." I noted.

"I have no plans to cause you harm. I just wanted to protect you from the actual threats that will come your way. If you agree to stay here for just a few days a week tops, I will tell you everything I know and I'll even help you understand and develop your gift if that is something you're interested in." Nuala tried to appease.

I sighed. "It doesn't really feel like I have much of a choice."

"You do. Either way, you will be returned as soon as it's safe to do so." She assured me.

My curiosity is peaked, so I agree.

13

So I have discovered that I am a mutant and my long since missing father was a mad scientist whom is to blame. Well, this is definitely not how I planned for my weekend to go. To make matters worse, I'm being held hostage in a way of sorts. I guess it's more of a temporary confinement that's isolated somewhere on the west-coast. Technically, I was kidnapped for my protection, to keep me from being kidnapped by a terrorist group that wants to use me as a weapon. Day two of my new weird life.

"Are you ready?" The red queen, Nuala, asked me.

"Am I ready for what?" I asked with curiosity. She is wearing black leggings and a black tank top. She looks like a ninja.

"Training. It's time we called out that untapped power. Let's see just how gifted you truly are." She replied with a devious smile. "Put this on. You won't be able to move in that dress." She added as she threw clothing similar to what she was wearing into my lap.

I changed as quickly as possible. I have to admit; I am very intrigued about what she has in store. What did she mean by training? How do you train someone to read memories? I guess I'll find out. They escorted me to an enormous room that had been emptied of all the furniture. Only blue padded mats are spread all over most of the floor. Giving the room the look of a dojo or gym. Like the rest of the house, the windows are blacked out. The red queen sat in the middle of the floor with her legs crossed, Lotus style. She motioned for me to join her and to do the same. There are six men standing along the walls. They are all armed. I sat down directly in front of her about three feet away. She motioned for me to come a little closer, and I did.

"Tell me Shontelle, what do you do to relax?" She inquired.

I had to think about that since I'm not a stressed out person. "When I feel a little anxious, I listen to classical music to clear my mind." I replied.

She looked towards a guard whom quickly left the room. "Have you ever tried meditation?" Nuala asked.

"No, I have never felt the need to be enlightened." I joked.

"You should try it. Some people find out so much about themselves after a good meditation. Some people even find inner peace." She sounds like a guru.

"So I have heard, although that sounds deep and spiritual. I am fine with who I am." I insist.

"That's just it. You're not being you, not really. You're just an exposed shell. The real you have yet to make an appearance. I plan to change that." The guard returned with a sound system similar to a karaoke machine. "Who's your favorite?" she asked

"Antonio Vivaldi." I told her as she walked over to the large speaker. After a few seconds, the four seasons played.

"Now I want you to sit as comfortably as possible and just relax. Take deep, slow breaths. Inhale and hold, now exhale." Nuala instructed. "Meditation is a technique that focuses the mind on a particular thought or activity to train attention awareness." I did as she said, primarily out of curiosity. I was very interested in seeing where this was going. "Now I want you to listen not with your ears, but with your mind. Channel your focus to the pull of your cerebral cortex. What do you hear?" Nuala asked.

"Just some crazy lady barking orders at me." I replied with a smile. Suddenly she grabbed my shoulders, the touch opened the floodgates of my mind. The memories poured in. I pulled away and looked at her in shock.

Nuala looked confused. Then she smiled. "So it's still in the beginning stages of manifestation, not fully developed."

"What do you mean?" I asked, gasping. I felt winded from the rush of memories bombarding through my mind.

"It means that we have a lot of work to do. Not knowing you had this gift makes it more work to bring it to full power. Let's try again." Nuala beseeched me.

"No, what was that?" I'm freaking out now. That overwhelming sensation was too much.

"That is your gift coming out. Do not fight it. I'm going to hold your hands and I want you to focus. Tell me what you see." Nuala motioned for me to come closer to her and reached her hands out to me. I took a deep breath and then grabbed her hands and tried to focus. What I saw moved quickly, like a movie. If I watched the movie being rewound, or at least that's how it seems.

Suddenly something caught my interest, and the movie played out. It is the red queen. When she arrived here, she came via helicopter. She is not alone. Nuala is talking to a small child maybe 3 or 4 years old. A girl with blonde hair and green eyes. The girl has to be her daughter. I can sense the love and the fear. Within a few seconds, the girl transforms into a large cat. A cougar with a unique brown spot on the left shoulder blade. I was being pulled back away from the memory and the little cougar girl.

"Shontelle, wake up. Are you alright?" I was lying back, looking up at the red queen.

"I'm fine. What happened?" My mind is racing as I try to focus and sit up.

"You became still. I was afraid you were having some type of seizure. Are you sure you're okay?" Nuala asked, her brow furrowed with worry.

"Yes, I'm fine. Am I the only one here? You know the only one like me?" I asked.

"Of course, why do you ask?" Nuala's eyes searched mine. Realization had her eyes widening comically before she asked, "What did you see?"

"The better question would be, who did I see?" She looked at me with a puzzled expression. I saw it as soon as it came to her?

"Did you see her?" she asked in a low voice.

"Who is she?" I asked. "And is she being held here against her will as well?" I could keep the anger out of my tone if I tried.

"She is well, and no, she isn't. She's just here for personal reasons. She's leaving tomorrow." Before I could ask her anything else, one guard offered me a cup with a cold liquid. I looked at him with suspicion.

"It's just iced tea." He assured me. To be sure, I grab his arm and focused in on him and his daily activity. I saw the Tea being given to him by a large man in the kitchen. He brought it straight here from there without tampering with it. I released his arm and took the Tea. He also left a full pitcher on a serving cart.

Wow, that was exceptional. That time, it just happened more naturally. I must admit, for some strange reason, I was becoming more intrigued. The red queen stood up and asked, "How well can you physically defend yourself?"

"About as well as you can, most likely, but I've never really needed to do so. My body may not agree with my intent." I admitted.

"Then let's get that body to remember. Have some tea first. It may help your muscle memory." Nuala advised as she stood up to stretch her joints.

I did as she suggested, and she was right. I almost instantly felt a burst of energy, not only energetic, but somehow relaxed as well. We did an easy stretch warmup, followed by yoga. She, of course, knew that I was in gymnastics for most of my childhood and had me show her my layouts. I think I impressed her. If not, I definitely impressed myself.

Standing directly in front of me, Nuala said, "Your body seems fit to me. Are you ready to get physical?"

Before I could reply, she swung her right fist, aiming for my head. I dodged, then I gave her my best roundhouse kick. It didn't land. Nuala moved swiftly and attempted to knock off my head with her foot. I quickly did a back flip out of her grasp. I also clipped her chin with my foot. She fell backwards, landing on her arse, and all the guards moved towards her, but she held up her hand, stopping them in their tracks.

"That was great. I underestimated you." She said while she was still trying to catch her breath.

"Most people do. I guess I forgot to mention that I had memorized a variety of self-defense training techniques and mixed martial arts." I took a step towards her offering my hand, pulling her up. Refilling my teacup, I finished the pitcher.

I was excited and curious, yet somehow, I'm still on edge about my current circumstances. I have so many questions. "So what is all of this for, and when can I leave?" I asked after my exasperation passed.

"Don't worry, it won't be much longer. I have arranged a ransom of sorts. You will be home in no time. I would like you to train with me for a few more days, and then I will send you home unharmed and prepared." She answered.

"What's in this tea? It's really invigorating." I confessed. Also asking, "And what exactly am I training for?"

"It's an old family recipe that I tweaked. An herbal concoction made to give energy and help to expand your mind." The red queen announced with pride.

"Well, I definitely want the recipe." I replied. "Great, so are we taking a break or what?" I inquired.

Nuala shook her head. "No, let's continue. How about you

show me some of what you can do?" After I demonstrated a little gymnastics, ballet and jujitsu, she allowed me to return to my room for some rest and relaxation. I am barely winded, but my mind is racing.

14

It has been five days since they kidnapped me or saved me from being kidnapped by a terrorist group. I think, I'm not sure, it's hard to keep track when everything is blacked out and there aren't any clocks. My calculations are based on my internal clock. Each day I've learned something new. Nuala spars with me for a couple of hours each day, sharing a few tips and techniques. She checks in with me regularly for progress reports on my gift development. Of course, I make sure to only share the bare minimum. For example, yesterday I told her I could search for memories faster and retain all the information. What I didn't tell her is that I no longer need physical contact. I also know exactly where I am. Unfortunately, I can't figure out how to escape with such heavy security. I've been able to piece together most of the real reason I'm here, and I believe it has more to do with my father than it is with me. It's still hard to tell if they're really trying to protect me or use me for their own diabolical scheme. There is a possibility that it's both.

When I'm alone, I try to push myself. I meditate and focus my kinetic energy around me. Unfortunately, every time I get close to a breakthrough, I pass out. The strange part is every time I pass out, my dreams don't feel like memories. I instantly feel like I'm someone else, as if I'm living *A Day in the Life* of someone else, but just for a few hours. It's different each time.

Once I was in a bathroom combing my hair and when I looked in the mirror, I was a middle-aged, middle eastern woman. After putting my hair into a braided ponytail, I made my way to an office and sat at a computer and then researched telepathic brainwaves and modern doctors' research on genetic mutation and manipulation. I came out of it before it went any further, but maintained the information for the future, just in case.

My theory is that I not only can read people's memories, but I can transfer my consciousness into their minds with almost a firsthand view of their lives. If I'm correct, I wonder how much more of their mind I can penetrate.

I guess Doctor Douglas wasn't that far off. I'm also hoping that my mind can communicate telepathically. I haven't actually been able to penetrate anyone's current thoughts. Sometimes the memories are actually dreams or fantasies and it can become complicated to differentiate. So far, each person has been unaware of my intrusion into their mind.

I also haven't figured out exactly how I even got so deep into their mind or how to stay awake when I do. Oh well, another lesson for another day.

My dad has somehow done the impossible and made me and my family into comic book characters. I wonder if they can do what I can or if it's different. Why did he keep this from me? He had to know that it would somehow affect me at some point. I wish he was here to explain himself. I hate that he's gone and never coming back. I miss him more than anything. Despite what happened when I was a stubborn child, I had always been a daddy's girl. My father was the only person who truly understood me. We had the same interests and dislikes. He was the only person in my world that I felt I could always be myself with. He always told me I would one day change the world. Maybe that was his subtle hint of what would become of me. Maybe my mom will have some answers for me. As soon as I am freed from this place, I will confront her and demand that she tell me everything.

First, I have to get out of here. If Nuala is telling the truth about saving me from the people that want to use me as some type of weapon for war. I would gladly keep in contact with her, but something is telling me to be cautious. How do I know who to trust?

In the room I've been using, there is a bookshelf. Textbooks on Herbology for biology, physics, medical theories through the ages, neuroscience, theories of evolution and one small picture book. This is out-of-place here. I grab the herbology book; I prefer it over reading physics equations. I enjoy reading but physics is almost a foreign language. I understand the math, but that's only because it's pre registered into my brain from high school and college. Being able to remember does not mean automatic knowledge and understanding. Sometimes it comes in steps. I remember the teachings of the professors or the notes, then I can process the information. Once I remember the steps, I can do the work easily. So it can sometimes take a few moments for me to process. Remembering isn't understanding, although math and science are my strengths. I prefer chemistry. That's why the current degrees I'm working on are biochemistry and cell and molecular biology, although it can change at any moment to microbiology. Getting dual doctorates was easy since I had absolutely no social life. Who knows what it will be in the end? After all of this, it might be genetics. My brother has a doctorate in neuroscience, yet he owns a restaurant. My mom has two masters and a doctorate, yet she has made the decision to be a trophy wife for a man she barely tolerates. I don't even think they sleep in the same room. My older sister has a bachelor's degree in fashion and merchandizing, yet she doesn't work at all. She just uses my parents as her own private Piggy Bank, especially my stepfather. Her lavish weekend in Santorini, Greece, had a bill that would make the average person faint and don't get me started with what happened in Maldives. I'll admit that

I'm not the most frugal person, but that type of lavish lifestyle has never been for me. I prefer comfort and knowledge.

Today seems a little off. There is literally something in the air. What is that smell? It's like a wet dog playing in a Rose Garden smell. I think I'm going to lose my breakfast and I don't think that oatmeal will taste any better the second time around.

Mario, the guard who has been bringing me most of my meals, came in to play a game of cards with me a few hours ago. According to him, I'm a hustler. He's not wrong. In the beginning, I would check his memory to track his hands, but it was just practice to see if I could without him noticing any changes in my behavior. Then I played fair, but he still loses because he just sucks at poker.

I'm not sure exactly how many days have passed, but he's come to keep me company a few times, once I'm done sparring with Nuala, always with a game in hand. He seems to have noticed the strange odor as well. "Stay here Ms. Spyce. I'll check out what's going on." he said, as if the option to leave my room was available to me. He returned shortly after and handed me the dress I had arrived in. "you need to get dressed. You will leave soon."

"Are you sure?" I jumped up from the small desk, my heart strumming.

"Yes, so get dressed and meet me in the Hall." he said before giving me privacy to change.

I dressed quickly. Once i was done, I walked out of my temporary room into the hallway. I looked to my left and saw three guards conversing. One was holding leather cuffs and a blindfold. Instead of fear, my mind took this moment to decide now would be the best time to think about the night I lost my virginity — kinky. I stood there waiting for Mario. He made his way towards me. Following my line of sight and said in a gentle voice, "Don't worry, I will make sure that you make it home safely. I just want you to know that I know you didn't have a choice, but I enjoyed my time with you. I hope to see you again in the real world. Maybe, We might even get to work together."

I gave him a smile and said, "I hope so, or atleast get the opportunity for me to teach you how to play a proper game of poker." I jested.

Mario's smile was the last thing i saw before everything went dark.

15

The helicopter ride is quite invigorating. I think being blindfolded and cuffed makes it feel almost like an amusement park ride. I'm pretty sure at this point that I have some type of sensory deprivation kink. I hope Adrian is into it. I am almost positive that Dorian would be. No, wait, I refuse to think about him. He is not the man for me. Just because he's been in my dreams doesn't mean that he is the man of my dreams. I want to point out that I know where I'm going and where we just left, but they don't need to know my gift's strength has intensified. I doubt that they'd be able to hear me, anyway. I am escorted through a vacant pier. After removing the blindfold and restraints, I am then guided to a bench at the end of the pier.

"Wait here and your family will come to get you in a few minutes." Nuala informed me.

"How do I get in touch with you? For future reference." I asked.

"Don't worry, we're never too far, but if you need us, just make a post involving an animal. We'll respond." She replied.

I scoffed. "You can't be serious. I don't have any pets."

"it doesn't have to be a pet. It could be a Meme or Gif. You never post anything with animals, so I'll know what it is. You should also know that your parents have been meeting with private security firms, so you have that to look forward to." Nuala taunted with a mischievous smile.

"Of course. Constant supervision from strangers sounds perfect for an introvert like me." I rolled my eyes.

Within five minutes of Nuala's departure. I saw my sister Julissa walking towards me. She's wearing an overly lavish all white couture pant suit and white, red bottom stilettos. Because why not?

"Oh my god, Shonnie are you ok? Did they hurt you?" she asked with mild concern and a quick hug.

"I'm fine. What are you doing here?" I asked with too much irritation echoing in my voice.

Julissa pulled away and said, "Your abductors sent multiple pickup locations, so we all split up to find you. I guess I picked the short straw. Do you have any idea how panicked mom is? I'll text them now and let them know you're with me."

"Thanks for coming for me. I know I'm not your favorite person." An understatement for sure. It's a known fact how much she loathes me.

"You don't have to be, your still my sister." Julissa made a few stops before getting to the manor. I guess to her, what happened wasn't a big deal. I stayed in the car and watched my surroundings. My mind is now on high alert.

Outside of the manor, there are armed security personnel monitoring the property as we made our way through the gates. "Just so you are aware, Ignatio's convinced mom to keep your abduction quiet from the media and local authorities. There aren't any that know what happened. Just the family and your friends that came with you."

"I'm sure it's for the best. I'd prefer my privacy, as they both know." I'm actually shocked by this information. My mom once called the FBI when I was 3 hours late coming home from a biology exhibition. I was twenty years old. I wonder how my step-father pulled that trick off.

Once I was inside the manor, Brandon immediately grasped

me in a massive bear hug. He swung me around and then turned me towards my weeping mother. I've never seen my mother so out of sorts. No makeup, a tracksuit, and hollowed eyes. It gives her a deathly look. Tears are pouring down her face. She clenched me to her, and I wrapped my arms around her, holding her tight, loving the familiar scent of her favorite hibiscus and cherry blossom shampoo. Giving her the comfort she and i both need.

I said, "I'm ok mom, they did not harm me, I'm just as I was a few days ago."

I pulled back and looked down at the petite beauty that brought me into this world. Even with her face bare and eyes hollowed, she still had stunning features. Her oval face, green eyes and jet black hair. Her normally pouty lips were quivering. I continued to reassure her as we walked into the family dining room. There is a small group of staff setting up for a buffet style lunch. Ignatios entered first and dismissed everyone. Sans four heavily armed security guards and a young man in a black and crimson tailored suit.

"Shontelle, we're so happy you're home? I'm Jace, the head of security. If you have any questions, feel free to contact me at anytime." He handed me a business card that was black on the front with an unfamiliar but interesting logo of a dragon eating an eagle pressed into it on one side and on the reverse it was red with his number and email written in black. Well, that's not disturbing at all. "Thanks, but I doubt I'll need it. I don't live here." "I'm aware. I have set your condo up with a top of the line security system for when you're ready to return." I looked around, dumbfounded. My mother held my hand and lead me to the chairs closest to us.

Once we were seated my mom spoke. "Shonnie sweetheart, I'd prefer that you stay here until this blows over. You'll be safe until we find the people who stole you."

"What do you mean, they let me go? Why would you go after them?" I tried to keep my voice calm, although my irritation was apparent.

"There is more to this than just some punks looking for a payday. I just want to make sure they don't come back looking for another one." She said.

"Do you know why I was targeted?" I asked, watching her response closely. Ignatios stood behind my mother, squeezing her shoulders, offering her comfort. "I'm sure some ex-cons just saw an opportunity and took it. All future events will have increased security details."

"I doubt this was a random act. Why me? They could have just as easily taken Julissa. She's far more well known than I am and there were other heiresses with far richer parents than me." I'm baiting her to see how much she really knows or how much she's willing to share with me.

"I don't know. Maybe they saw you alone and saw an opportunity." She replied, not giving me any eye contact.

"Or maybe something else entirely is going on and I'm being left completely in the dark." I hissed.

My mother looked at me shell-shocked. "What are you implying, Shontelle?"

"I'm not implying anything. I just find it odd that I was coerced to attend this party and somehow you believe I was just randomly kidnapped for a quick payday. It seemed thoroughly planned to me." I stated.

"What did they do to you?" She queried, now looking me straight in the eyes.

"Nothing, absolutely nothing. That's just it. That's what makes this feel like it wasn't just something random." I admitted.

My mother worried her lip and looked up at my stepfather, almost questioning. Perhaps she didn't know what to say.

Ignatios found the words for her. "We have investigators looking into what happened. We will find them and take care of it." His attempt to reassure me sounds more nefarious than comforting.

16

There is absolutely no way im going to stay here. How could they not realise that being under lock and key with a guard at my door doesn't make feel safe in the slightest? I'm just reliving the past week. Besides being able to leave my room and roam freely on the property, I'm still stuck somewhere I don't want to be. I need to get the hell out of here. As I try to devise a plan to escape my current circumstance, there is a knock at my door.

"Shonnie it's me." my mom announced through the door

"Come in mom."

"i just wanted to check in on you and see how you are doing?"

"I can't say that im okay with everything going on right now, but I'll be fine, im sure."

"Of that, I am sure." She said, smiling as she came in and sat on the chaise on the left side of my bed.

"Mom, I can't stay here with the armed forces. I feel like im being held against my will." I complained.

"I know, sweetheart Ignatios is just being overprotective. He feels terrible about what happened he blames himself. If he wouldn't have pressured you to come." She pointed out.

"How could he have known what would happen?" I replied.

"He still feels terrible about what happened. He just wants to make sure you remain safe." My mother acknowledged.

I sighed. "I will agree to a bodyguard for the time being, but I don't need an entire special forces team." I stated.

"I'll talk to step-father about it."

"Mom, I need to go back to my place today. I do still have school and my final thesis is due soon. I was only able to get one turned in." I confessed.

"I'll make it happen if I can." She said.

"Thanks."

My mom made her way to the door and paused. Without looking at me, she hesitated for a moment. "If you want to talk about anything that has happened, I will always be available to you, no matter what. So if you need to purge or even ask questions, let me know." Her tone was distinct, as if there was something else that she was trying to convey.

"When I'm ready, you will be the first person I turn to, but not right now."

She turned and looked at me knowingly. "All I want is to go home. Can you make that happen?"

"You can go home. We're just trying to get your security team setup." she stated.

"I don't need a team of security. I just need maybe one or two. Please don't make this into a shit show, mom." I chided.

"Fine, you can leave within the next forty-eight hours. You'll be informed when it's time. Also, your friend Dahlia's here. Would you like me to send her up?" She informed me.

"Yes. I would appreciate that." I sat on the end of my childhood bed and flopped back, only to shoot back up as the door abruptly burst open with a frantic Dahlia.

"Spyce what the hell, are you ok? Did they hurt you?" she sat beside me and grasped me by my shoulders, jerking me towards her in a fierce hug.

I gasped, "It's a long story but I'm ok. No harm came to me while I was gone."

"Thank heavens, I was panicked out of my mind. I was sure you left the party while Brandon and I... umm... were talking." She stumbled to find the proper words. "Since no one saw you, I assumed you snuck out and went home, so I had Brandon take me. You weren't there either, but Dorian was. It freaked him out. He said that he came back for the same reason. We all returned here and talked to your step dad. After making your mom aware, they shut down the party, checking everyone's cars as they left the property. After a full sweep of the manor, your mother became frantic. Everyone tried your cell at some point, but it went straight to voicemail. I found your purse and cell in the garden."

She went into more details about what they found and that she and Dorian were asked to go home once they were sure I was nowhere to be found. Just in case i found my way back home.

"Shonnie there was an incident between Adrian and Dorian while you were gone. I know that you're into Adrian and that's Fine. It's just Dorian made a good point that he was the last one to see you and he left pretty early. It's almost as if he just wanted to make sure you were here."

I gave her an incredulous look.

"I'm not saying this was his doing, but maybe he knows something that we don't. He made sure his little sister wasn't here. Maybe it was in case things didn't go as planned." She proposed.

"Is that what Dorian said?" I asked.

"It was what he said right after he slammed his fist into Adrian's face." She confessed.

"What the hell did he do that for?" I probed, awestruck.

"My brother might be an insufferable flirt, but he's very protective of those he cares for." She replied.

"And you believe he cares for me? Why? He doesn't even know me. I'm not that important." I pointed out.

"Do me a favor and don't say that in front of Dorian. I know him well enough to know that he cares about you, although he has a piss poor way of showing it. He wouldn't approve of your self assessment." Dahlia acknowledged.

"I guess I'll have to reassure him that Adrian had nothing to do with what happened." I diverted the subject. "I'm going to tell you something that's going to sound completely outrageous, but I need you to trust that I'm telling you the truth. Just as I'm trusting you and only you with this information." I trust Dahlia more than anyone else, and I can't keep everything to myself. I tell her everything from the crazy mad science of my family's past to the potential chaos in our future.

Once Dahlia stopped laughing and snorting like an insane cartoon pig, she looked me in my eyes and saw the truth of what I was telling her. "Wait, you're serious? This isn't a joke."

"I don't think I'm that creative." I replied.

She took a moment to contemplate. "Okay, read my mind. What am I thinking of right now?"

I laughed softly. "That's not how it works. I can't actively read your thoughts, but I can see your memories as recent as the last two minutes."

"I'm sorry Shonnie, But I'm going to need some type of demonstration?" She's grinning at me with an arched eyebrow.

I decide seeing is believing for her, so I focus on her mind. I sift through her most recent memories and reach for something that I couldn't possibly know. I stop finding what I'm looking for, not going through too much, for my own comfort.

"It's weird that I'm just putting together that you and Brandon are a thing. Especially how obvious you guys have been. Do you always go to Wizard con, together, or was this the first meet up? I guess you couldn't resist his Dumbledore costume, Hermione Granger. Talk about an age gap romance." I smile as her face immediately drops and her eyes widen in sheer horror.

"Oh. My. Gosh. You're a freaking psychic!" She squeals and then clears her throat, trying to compose herself. "By the way, he wasn't Dumbledore, he was Gandalf the gray." We both broke into hysterical laughter. Once we regained our composure, she grabbed my hand and squeezed. "I want you to know that no matter what's going on or what happens, I'll always be there for you. I'm your ride or die. That will make these other bitches cry. No matter what, I'm on your side."

I smiled at her, knowing she means every word. Finding that one friend you can trust wholeheartedly is rare and almost an impossible feat. I will always be thankful for having her in my life. I may not have realized how amazing she is right away, but I'm sure of it now.

There's a knock on my door and we both look towards it. I tell the person to come in, not asking who it is.

Adrian steps in, leaving the door cracked. "I just wanted to see if I could have a moment to talk to you?" The question sounded hesitant coming out. The uncertainty in his eyes was clear. Obviously what happened and Dorian's accusations have put him on edge.

"I was just on my way downstairs. Your brother and mom promised me some amazing crepes?" She smiled at me before she made her way out of my childhood room. Closing the door softly behind her.

17

Adrian sat beside me on my childhood bed. His dark blonde hair neatly pulled away from his face. His goatee is perfectly trimmed. He placed his hands on my shoulders and massaged inwards towards my neck. The tension inside lessened immediately, and I let out a sigh. It's funny that he just went straight in, knowing exactly what I needed. My headache even subsided. He pulled my body into his and kissed my forehead. "I know you have a lot of things weighing on you, but you have to remember to take a moment and just breath. Take control and remember that you hold all the power over your life."

"Thank you." I whispered.

He smiled and said, "I just want you to do what's best for you, even if it ruffles a few feathers."

I looked up into Adrian's eyes and asked, "What made you come back to California? Was it something specific?"

"Nothing more than I missed it. I know boring, the weather is outstanding and I have a few businesses here. After my father passed away, I felt compelled to pick up his mantle. I also thought it would be cool to be a young and successful entrepreneur in the land of hot models and actresses. After a month or two, it got old." He explained.

"So, just business and pleasure?" I asked to confirm.

He smirked at me, leaning in close to my ear. "I learned what genuine pleasure was the more that I spent time with you."

Oh yeah, he's good. I felt my face light up at his proclamation.

He continued. "I know we've had some casual conversations and I've learned some basic things about you, but I want to get to know the real you. I want to see the Shontelle every one overlooks, the person you keep guarded for safekeeping."

"It's never been easy for me, socially I feel like an outcast. I am often treated as if my mind and body shouldn't coexist. I've been called pretty, but weird. To smart for my face. Do you know I lost my virginity just to scratch an itch, so to speak? I wanted it to be more, but I could not get one person to see me. All of me and accept the real me. No male or female could fully accept me for who I am. I was just too weird. So in my first year of grad school, I asked my roommate to help me have a one-night stand."

The look on Adrian's face is priceless. Dropped jaw and wide eyes. After helping him pick his jaw up off the floor, I continued. "The guy doesn't even know my name and I don't know his or even what he looks like."

Adrian interrupted me, "Wait. How is it you don't know what he looks like?"

I straightened up and looked down at my hands as I ran them over my dress, smoothing it out. "I asked to be blindfolded." I announced.

Adrian looked floored. His eyes widened. "Why? Is it because looks weren't important, just doing the deed and getting it over with?"

As feasible as his question was, it was only partially the reason. "No, nothing like that. It was because, good or bad, it would be permanently etched into my brain. I wasn't sure how it would turn out and I didn't want to risk a bad memory I couldn't get rid of."

"So you don't really remember it?" Adrian asked.

"Memories are stronger for me when they are visual. Imagine

if it was terrible, and I kept playing it over on repeat like it was still happening. Or what if the guy is someone I see regularly and seeing him keeps it in the forefront of my mind?"

"Was it Terrible?" He inquired.

The look on Adrian's face was serene, yet I could sense agitation simmering below the surface. Telling him how I wish every day that I could identify who I lost my virginity to. That I sometimes fantasize about it when I'm home alone in my bed. When I think about how careful and cautious he had been with me. How he took his time as he caressed and tasted every part of my body. He had made me climax multiple times and sent my body into a euphoric state. It felt like I had merged my soul into his. When it was over and he had left. I felt like I lost a part of myself, maybe my soul or heart. I couldn't be sure. Maybe a bit of both. Either way, that night still is permanently etched in my memory without the visuals. Sometimes I can get a hint of his scent. Now and then I get a familiar feeling, like he's watching me from a distance.

I sighed. "No, not terrible, just another thing from the past that will stay there."

"Was that your only time?" Adrian's curiosity was telling.

"No, I took a chance with someone I found attractive. Twice and altogether, he lasted six minutes and I wish I could get that time back. He only wanted to get his, if you know what I mean. After that, I figured I can do better to give my body what it needed on my own. Perhaps euphoria is an once In a lifetime deal," I replied exasperated.

"For some, not for you, though I'm sure of that. Maybe the right person will help bring you back to it. Just give them some time." Adrian brushed a stray curl behind my ear and slid his hand down my neck. His thumb grazed along my jaw and he leaned in and brushed his lips over mine. I pushed my lips into his with a little more pressure, trying to deepen the kiss. He let me take over, and I wanted all of It even the breath from his body. His mouth was sensually enticing. It brought me back to that night. Only the guy who kissed me then took control of the kiss with dominance and precision. Adrian placed a hand on the back of my head, cradling it in place. I wrapped my arms around his torso, trying to pull his body as close to mine as possible, if not closer. I wanted to feel his hard rippled muscles against my soft curves.

He chuckled at my intensity. His lips brushed against my cheek, neck, and collarbone. His fingers were sliding down my spine, leaving a trail of sensuous pleasure straight to my core. He leaned into me demurely, guiding me back into the mattress beneath us. The moment was sensual, and he was cautious, being insanely gentle, as if he was afraid I may shatter underneath the weight of him. His delicate kiss is maddening. I'm not sure of how much more I can handle of this precarious moment. I took back control of the kiss with an immense intensity. My fingers intertwined behind his neck, pulling him into me, deepening the kiss. He reacted instantly, losing his gentle teasing. Adrian gripped my hair just tight enough to get my attention as he pulled his mouth from mine, only to place them to the nape of my neck. His hands rove frantically all over my body, exploring, leaving a trail of heat and delight. My breath hitched once his lips, along with his tongue, traveled down my sternum to the top of my breast. I ran my fingers through his hair as my body arched into him. His fingers slid my top's spaghetti straps down my shoulders, freeing my breast as his mouth devoured my aching brown peaks. I gripped his hair tighter, not wanting him to stop. A soft knock at the door caused us to freeze.

Adrian looked up into my eyes, almost pleading for me to send whoever it is a way. My mind was racing, and I almost forgot where I was for a moment. As if seeing the answer in my eyes, Adrian pulled himself back, casually pulling me up with him. I righted myself quickly, informing the person to enter.

Dorian opened the door with a smile on his face that pulled at my heart with all the relief it held. That smile dissipated the instant he saw Adrian sitting beside me on my bed, adjusting his pants. His eyebrows furrowed, eyes blazing with flames that emitted a heat that permeated through to my soul. Drawing his gaze away from Adrian, I stood, reaching my hand out towards him, beckoning him towards me. Dorian shifted his stance, turning his gaze towards me. Although his anger was palpable, his eyes softened the moment they returned to me.

"I came here as soon as Dee told me you were back. I needed to see that you were ok for myself." I could feel all the blood rushing to my face as

I lowered my head, trying to hide how his concern affected me. Dorian's simple presence always seems to send a sense of awareness throughout my entire body, causing my blood to heat as it flowed straight to my core. Dorian's arms wrapped around my waist, pulling me into an embrace. He held me tightly, causing my breast to press tightly against his firm chest. That heat in my core too turned into an inferno.

"I'm fine. Thank you for checking in on me." I whispered into his neck.

"I will always look out for you, no matter what. If you need me, I'll be there." Dorian placed a gentle kiss on my forehead. The comforting warmth caused me to close my eyes, and I clenched my thighs, trying to keep the impending flood at bay.

"Does your mom know you're here?" Dorian suddenly snapped at Adrian. interrupting our sensual moment with his anger that broke me from his alluring spell.

"I'm twenty-six years old. I don't have to report in to my 'mommy', about my whereabouts. Does your dad know where you are?" Adrian replied vehemently.

I backed away cautiously, standing to the side, giving a wide berth between the three of us.

"I doubt it, seeing how you should be halfway across the world.

Tell me, did you come back to treat a peculiar itch between your legs or did you find something crawling up your ass?" Adrian mocked.

My head swung back and forth between them as they took barbs at each other. The irony that we are standing in a literal triangle is not lost on me. Confusion and then curiosity take a hold of me.

"You insufferable asshole, I...." I stepped in between them, interrupting Dorian before this got physical. My child hood room doesn't need to become a crime scene and my collectibles will be useless if they're covered in blood splatter. The look on Dorian's face was homicidal. Adrian's was just as murderous in a creepy, nonchalant way. I wasn't aware that these two new each other so well. I had assumed that they only knew of each other because of their paths crossing because of me. I obviously am missing vital information.

"Can someone please explain to me what is going on here? How do you guys know each other exactly?" I implored.

Dorian's jaw clenched, and his fist balled firmly at his sides. Giving a sinister look that raised the hairs on the back of my neck.

Adrian replied. "Our parents are married."

"Separated, actually." Dorian interjected.

The thickness of the tension in the room was suffocating despite its vast space. I got a taste of claustrophobia. After swallowing deeply and taking in deep, calculated breaths, I calmly turned to Dorian. His gaze locked on Adrian. I took a step towards him, gliding my hands to his wrist. He unclenched his fist and redirected his attention back to me. His anger seemed to disperse instantly.

"I'll see you when you get back home, but for now, I'll let you get some rest." With a possessive bear hug, a kiss on the cheek and a threatening glare towards Adrian, Dorian retreated from our presence.

"Should I be concerned?" Adrian took cautious steps behind me as I stared off towards the closed door. Breaking my trance, I spun, guiding my attention where it should have always been.

"No more than I should be of your sister." I assured him. He stepped back to my bed, pulling me along with him as he took a seat. I stood in front of him. Adrian coaxed me down into his lap. Placing one hand on the small of my back and the other above my knee. Waiting for me to pick up where we left off before Dorian's interruption.

"As much as I hate to admit it, I am exhausted now that the adrenaline has died down. Can we meet up later after I've had some time to rest and regenerate some of my energy that you surely will help me exert?"

Adrian flashed that gorgeous smile at me. "Of course we can. I'm still staying with Brandon, so let me know when you get home. I'll come check on you then." Lifting me as he stood, he turned with me cradled in his strong, muscular arms. Laying me gently on the mattress as he gave me a soft, sensual kiss that spiked my heart rate before exiting from my room.

Adrian stood in front of me to the right while Dorian stood directly across from him, but behind me. I hope they aren't here to get me to choose one of them because that would be an impossible decision. One I've been debating for days, but my greed and need for them both want them to be okay with sharing.

Adrian approaches me and crooks his finger under my chin and lifts it so that I look up at him. His eyes are glowing emeralds, inviting me into the emerald city where the wizard wielding them will fulfill my every aching need.

I turn my head slightly to the left as I feel Dorian's warmth against my back, his hands on my hips. They look at each other as if confirming a synchronized attack and then they do. Adrian presses his lips to mine as Dorian nips at the sensitive skin of my neck. They both use their tongues. Adrian licks at my top lip, a silent request that I willingly oblige. His tongue plays tag with mine and my brain instantly sends a pulsing alert to the apex of my thighs.

Dorian tastes my skin, licking and kissing a trail across my neck to the center. Continuing down my back slowly, making a warm wet path down my spine. Adrian's hands and mouth trail down my stomach as Dorians trail back up my spine. They each reach their destination as they remove my shorts and top. The coordinated attack continues as they toss my bra and panty.

Adrian continues to kiss me as his hand cups my vulva, rubbing his palm back and forth against the tiny bundle of nerves as he slides two of his fingers into my wetness, causing me to whimper.

Dorian's arms are both wrapped around my torso as he firmly squeezes both of my breast, one clutched in each hand. His muscle rippled, chest pressed against my back, and his firm steel grinding into my cheeks. He continues to place hot wet, kisses all over my back. He trails down to the base of my spine and then growls as he bites me on my left ass cheek. I gasp and Adrian groans into my mouth as his thumb rubs small circles over my clit.

Dorian, now kneeling behind me, spreads me wide and feasts. My breath catches and I lean into Adrian, holding on to his shoulders. Adrian holds me steady for a moment before breaking our tongue tango. He then also kneels in front of me. Leaving a trail of kisses down the front of my body, suckling each of my nipples before continuing his journey, planting kisses all the way down my thighs and up again. I shivered the moment his mouth was on my swollen nub.

I'm drenched.

Adrian slid those two thick fingers inside of me and my legs trembled. Together they both gripped a thigh, keeping me spread open for them as they continued to devour me.

My hands squeezed Adrian's shoulders tight as Dorian's thumb toyed with my tight puckered hole, slowly pressing inside. I screamed and convulsed as my release gushed freely.

I tried to catch my breath and balance as they both stood. Adrian kissed me demurely, and I could taste myself on his lips and tongue. He turned me so that I faced Dorian, who is now sitting at the top of my bed, completely naked. He crooks his finger at me while stroking himself. My eyes penetrate his perfectly toned and lean body. I practically drool at the sight of his thick, long, and proud cock. I crawl onto the mattress towards him, and Dorian leans in and gives me a tantalizing kiss.

I look into those honey gold eyes and decide I want to see how good he tastes. Without breaking eye contact, I grip his cock and instantly worry if it will even fit into my mouth. I lick the threatening drool from the corner of my lips. I'll happily unhinge my jaw just to fit him inside my mouth. I licked the tip and tasted his salted caramel. He tastes so good; I engorged myself. Sucking him down greedily, he grunts every time he hits the back of my throat. I take slow breaths through my nose like I'm snorkeling. I take him as deep as I can, drooling down the length of him. His hands tangle in my hair, not pushing or trying to control me, but just to hold on. Once again, I'm soaking wet, my cunt throbbing and leaking from the sounds coming from his sexy mouth. I feel Adrian kiss my back and slide his fingers between my folds, spreading my wetness over my hard clit. I look back and see his body completely hunched over me from behind. I can feel his thick cock pressed at my entrance. He rubs it against my clit and spreads my wetness all over his tip before he slowly fills me up. A loud moan escapes me.

Dorian, now on his knees, guides his cock back into my mouth. They both thrust slowly, testing me to see how much I can handle. I want more and I want it harder. I thrust back hard into Adrian while slurping Dorian like he's a melting popsicle. They both pump harder and deeper, in perfect synchronization. We all pant heavily, the sound echoing in a melody with the sound of slapping skin. Dorian has a tight hold on my hair and neck, while Adrian tightly grips my hips as they slam hard and deep into me, skewering me. my orgasm hits me hard and I gag as Dorians' cum shoots down my throat. I swallow it all down, sucking him dry, not stopping until I have devoured every single drop. Only then do I release him from my mouth. He leans down and kisses me as Adrian pummels me from behind, chasing his own release, filling me up completely with his ecstasy.

I woke up in a cold sweat, with a throbbing pulse and moisture coming from between my thighs. The intensity of that dream has caused a desperate and unreasonable, not to mention impossible, need to swell inside of me. I opted to feed a more satiable hunger. With my throat dry and stomach rumbling, I made my way downstairs to the kitchen.

It's early, and the house is eerily quiet. The hall lights are dimmed just enough to avoid complete darkness. As I make my way through the family room, my mother is sitting at the breakfast bar spaced out, looking through the window nursing a mug of coffee.

"Some ones up early. Good morning." I announced.

"Morning, technically I'm up late. I haven't gone to bed yet." She replied.

"Are you still rattled about my disappearance?" I asked.

"Yes, but it's more than that." She stated offhand.

I grabbed a mug and made myself some Jasmine and hibiscus tea as my breakfast croissant sandwich heated in the toaster oven.

"Would you care to elaborate?" I'm not sure what I'm expecting her to say, but I'm sure she has to be contemplating if she should tell me the truth or not.

"It's just some minor marital issues. We are having some disagreements." She continued staring out the window, not once giving me the slightest hint of her attention being on me. She hasn't looked my way once. My frustration is past the boiling point.

"Really, is it because of the security team or all the secrets?" I snapped in a loud whisper. Her focus was no longer on whatever was so damn important outside of that window. No, her attention is all mine now.

"What secrets exactly are you referring to?" She was facing me head on from the other side of the breakfast bar. Despite her shorter height, her glare was fierce and focused on me. Still, I refuse to relent.

"Wow, are there really that many? Just how many do you have? Just how much are you hiding from me?"

"What makes you even think I'm hiding anything from you?" She sounds confused, but she looks defensive. She has to know that I know.

"What do you imagine happened while I was being held captive? Do you think they tied me up and left me in the basement with no food and no water? Did I look distraught and destroyed when I got back? I wasn't. It wasn't even hard to be there. I Actually found myself in good company, although I don't entirely trust them, but to be honest I'm not exactly sure who to trust at this point. So many secrets. Which means so many lies. Are you finally ready to come clean to me about who I am, or should I say, what I am?"

My mother's face became completely bewildered. I ate my breakfast while she fought for the right words to say.

She asked me, "Do you know who took you and why?"

I studied her for a moment before replying. "I don't know them and I had never seen or heard of them before. I only know what they told me and things I established on my own."

"Would you like to share that information with me, including what you established of your own volition?"

I stared at her for a moment before laying my head down on my arms. Maybe I should have had coffee instead of tea.

"I am beyond exhausted. Just forget everything I said." I closed my eyes, but I can hear her soft footsteps coming towards me.

My mom gently brushed the tight curls away from my face, and I didn't look at her. "Tell me Shonnie, what would you like to know?"

"The woman that kidnapped me told me some rather elaborate stories about our family. To put it lightly, she all but made dad into a mad scientist that experimented on himself and his colleagues trying to save your life." I told her as I continued to rest my head, leaving my eyes closed.

"When the time is right, we will tell her, but as for now, I doubt the finders will even notice her. Brandon has been great with his discretion, especially for a five-year-old. no one is looking for us. We are an entirely different family now. The Sabry family no longer exists. When they died, the Spyce family was born."

My father stood in front of my mom as she sat bouncing her right leg nervously. While cradling a newborn baby swaddled in a tan cashmere blanket. "We have three kids now."

"Exactly. they will look for a family of three or four, if they think Brandon survived. A family of five would have been impossible in their minds. No one would believe another child could be possible. I'm not even sure how it was possible. She is our little gift. We are safe and I will always make sure we are. No matter what happens, you guys will always be safe." My father, Pharaoh, looked down into a pair of tiny silver orbs just like his and smiled.

My head shot up, almost clipping my mother's chin. "Who are the Sabrys?" My mother froze instantly. She was so stiff I couldn't tell if she was breathing.

To my relief, she spoke. "Where did you hear that name?" Her voice was panic-stricken.

"Who are they?" I insisted, now alarmed.

My mom held tightly to both of my hands with hers and asked more vehemently. "Shontelle, where exactly did you hear that name?"

"It just came up in my memory."

"That's impossible. That name was practically burned out of existence before you were born."

"Dad said it to you when I was a baby,"

"How could you remember? I was just thinking….. can you read minds, Shontelle?" her eyes were open wide. "Have you been reading my mind this whole time?"

"I don't know about that, but I have an excellent memory bank unlike you, if you forgot that."

"I know, but you were only three weeks old the last time that name was ever mentioned."

"Did dad do something to them? Are we in danger? Is that why someone tried to kidnap me?" My heart is racing and I am becoming consumed by panic.

"Listen to me, sweetheart. Now is not the best time for this discussion. Maybe you should go get ready for the day and I will talk to you about this later. We both have a lot of emotions to process because of recent events." with that statement, she hurried off and in less than sixty seconds later, Ignatios walked in and heads straight towards the coffeepot in the kitchen. "Good morning. Did you and your mom stay up all night or are you guys just early risers? She looked exhausted."

"I guess you could say that I'll be in my room." I mumbled. Since when does he get up at six a.m to get his own coffee? I've heard him beg my mom to get it every time the staff were off duty. He definitely doesn't wake up bright and early if he doesn't have work. Heck, on most days, he doesn't even get to work on time.

20

I can't tell if I'm losing my mind or if my powers are growing. Maybe my over active imagination has forced its way to the forefront of my mind. Fantasy merged into reality with a dab of possibility. Differentiating what's real and what's not is giving me a splitting headache.

A soft tap at my bedroom door interrupts my mental breakdown. Slowly opening as my mother peeked in.

My mother's soft voice cautiously filling the room. "Shonnie, May I come in?" I nodded and returned my attention to my desk. I leaned against it instead of sitting in the chair. I instead offered it to her. My mother sits and looks up at me. Her slight frame and short stature make her look delicate and innocent. Of course I know better. My mother isn't the docile woman I've known all my life. Hell, she's probably a superhero, or better yet, a supervillain for all I know.

"Shonnie I know you have millions of questions. What you need to know is that everything that happened before you and your brother were born was supposed to stay in the past. Your father and I were just trying to protect our family. For reasons such as what has happened of late. I never imagined that anyone would find out our kids have also become affected by the serums that were administered amongst us all those years ago."

"Don't you mean the serum dad created? Did you know what was going to happen?" I asked.

"I suspected, but there wasn't any way to be sure without running more test. Your father and I didn't want to take the risk of running test and having the results discovered. We already knew that our family was being monitored. That's why you and your brother were conditioned to avoid being in the spotlight. We didn't want to risk being discovered. Brandon was the first to show any signs. Once he did, your father talked to him and trained him to control it. You showed no signs of anything to cause concern. Being a genius just seemed relatively normal compared to what he was capable of. At least it did to me. Your father believed that there was more to you than met the eye. I guess he was right." She surmised.

"I think about him sometimes, wondering what happened. What if he died because of the people trying to come after me? Maybe he's dead because of me." I can't shake the feeling of guilt that latches itself to me each time I think about him. My father wasn't a saint by any means, but he loved and cared for us.

My mother had a mournful look when she spoke next. "I knew your father well, better than anyone. He definitely would do anything to protect his family. Whatever happened to your father was not your fault. The only wrongdoing on your part is blaming yourself for the things out of your control. Your father loved all of us."

"Maybe if he loved us a little less, he'd be alive." I pointed out.

"Your father saved my life and your brothers. In your quick history lesson of our family, was it mentioned that when I feel ill that I was pregnant with your brother? I bet not. No one knew except your Father and I. I had found out two weeks after my diagnosis. I believe that was also a boost of motivation for your father to find a cure. Which he did. No one ever envisioned what would come from it." She said.

"So what so-called gift were you blessed or cursed with?" What I have learned so far makes it feel like more of a curse, and the price was a life for a life. My father paid that price by playing God and, in the end, he is lost to those who loved him the most.

"My gift, as you call it, is regeneration and rapid healing. With Focus and physical contact, I can heal others. It's also possible that I age slower now. Most people just assume I've had work done. The truth is, I've looked the same since I was thirty. We lied about our age to everyone, even you kids. We said we were teen parents, but I was thirty-four when I had you." She told me.

I've always said that my mom looked more like she was my sister than my parent.

"Wait, so that would make you fifty-six on your next birthday. Is that even your real birthday?" I asked sarcastically.

"Yes, the first of March is my true birthday. The year was just changed." My mom assured me.

"So, did anything bad come from what happened to you? Like were there any negative side effects?"

She had a meek smile when she replied. "You mean besides being coerced by the government and hiding our true selves from the world? Your father kept them at bay for years. He changed everything about who we were. Our physical appearances had altered somewhat, because of the serum, so those of us that took it aren't so easily recognized from that time. It's almost as if we had become our best possible versions of ourselves. Our aging slowed, posture straightened, vision cleared, skin and eyes brightened, and scars disappeared. We became far more durable and immune to any illness. We also gained more strength in our body and senses."

I looked at her incredulously.

"You're essentially immortal. Like a vampire just without the ridiculous side effects, like bloodlust or spontaneous combustion in sunlight." I taunted sarcastically.

"You realize you have these same traits embedded in your DNA, right? You've never noticed that you always have a perfect physical and have never been to the emergency. You've never had the sniffles, or any known allergies. You were always the best at any sport and hardly even broke a sweat?"

"You barely let me do any sports after I was ten." I jokingly accused.

"That was just to avoid suspicion after Brandon took a baseball going ninety miles per hour to the head and the ball exploded. He tried to pretend to be injured, but there was no bruising or knots. We made the decision that it would be best to keep to the more simple solitary activities like your gymnastics and ice skating."

"I hate to disappoint you, but Julissa is always sick or suffering from something, and I just had a mild concussion a few weeks ago." I never got around to letting her know what happened on my first date with Adrian. The look on my mom's face didn't change.

"You didn't have a concussion. You had a triggered reaction to your gift."

"How could you possibly know that? Did Brandon tell you what happened?"

"No, he did not. Doctor Douglas did. Despite what you think, Doctor Douglas is an old friend. He was your pediatrician and our family Doctor because he knows about us and has kept our secret. As for your sister, she's different because she was born a year before everything happened. She wouldn't be as you would say 'Gifted' like us."

That makes sense. Julissa is inept. She is more like a functioning zombie that isn't decaying. Well, no more than a normal human.

"I appreciate you explaining things to me." I told her with all sincerity.

"It shouldn't have taken me this long, but after what happened with your father, I didn't want you to be fearful or go looking into the past. You already have so many insecurities I didn't want you to feel weird or like an outcast." She conveyed.

"I don't think you've been paying attention. If that was your main concern." I laughed. "It's ok, I know now and we can move forward."

"You're right. Let's get you back to your place and if you have more questions, stop by anytime. Just try to avoid discussing things in public or on the phone. Stay aware of your surroundings. Use your natural instincts and talents to stay safe." I hugged my mom tightly before she vacated my room.

21

The ride home couldn't have gone more smoothly. It was quick and efficient. Ignatios finally gave in and called of the military militia. I agreed to having four personal guards who will rotate in teams of two every twelve hours precariously. I've met each of them and so far they have shown the illicit skills of reconnaissance and Camoflauge. They're around Brandon's age, dress casually, and blend in with our surroundings.

Still, the idea of being monitored at all times drives me up the wall. I've never been one for exhibitionism. The only person in my family that actually enjoys a good spotlight is Julissa and most of the time, it proves to be unkind to her.

I make my way into the elevator with Harper and Collin, my two new shadows. Harper is a tall, gorgeous brunette with pale skin and dark brown eyes that can pierce deep into your soul, or at least that's how it feels to me. She is stunning and her insanely athletic body is amazing.

Collin is just as attractive, with his jet black hair pulled back in a neat ponytail and tight muscles. His arms are the size of my head. He looks like J Hope from BTS if he had a baby with Dwayne Johnson. Despite both of their beauty, their fuckoff faces will definitely keep anyone from approaching. The introvert in me loves it, but the experimental socialist is not sure how to move forward. That's a problem for another day.

I make my way into my apartment to find a seriously heated make-out session taking place on the love seat under the window. I quickly turn around facing the now closed door and loudly clear my throat once I realized it's Dahlia straddling my brother topless. I hear rustling and giggling as they try to get themselves together. "I guess I should have let you know I was on my way home."

"This was my fault. I didn't think mom would let you out of her sight and I convinced Dee." Brandon explains.

Dahlia scoffed. "More like pounced on me like a Puma."

"TMI, Dee." Brandon bumps his elbow into my arm. "The coast is clear."

I turn around smiling, then walk into the kitchen and grab a bottle of water before reconsidering and grabbing the Tennessee Whiskey and a glass tumbler from the cabinet. Dahlia follows me, grabbing two more tumblers. I take a seat on the less tainted couch, pouring my drink before setting the bottle on the coffee table.

Brandon grabs the bottle and pours two double shots before handing one two Dahlia. Gently caressing her back, he takes a sip from his glass.

Dahlias right knee bounced nervously, "So, surprise. Are you mad?"

I looked at her with a brow raised in confusion. "Why exactly would I be mad?"

She looks flustered and almost as confused as I am about her question. Brandon moved his hand from her back, placing it on her knee, giving it a slight squeeze. Answering for her, "She was concerned that you wouldn't approve after the reaction Julissa gave at the party." I was still confused.

"Well, as we all know, Julissa can be quite the pain in the ass, but I don't know what exactly you thought I would be upset about. You two are free to do whatever you want as consenting adults and you obviously have had a crush on Brandon for a while. I mean, for at least a year, according to my observations." Dahlia's eyes widened, and her jaw dropped at my declaration. Brandon leaned into her wearing the biggest smile with his green eyes shining bright. He kissed her cheek demurely and her mouth closed while her face relaxed.

"Yeah, Dee, it was only obvious. especially when you only wanted to go to tour Europe because you couldn't handle seeing him with that scrawny harlot, as you called her." Dorian's voice came from the hallway before he made it into the living room.

"I never called her that." Dahlia exclaimed defensively, facing Brandon, who was still smiling.

"She was skinny and cheating on me, so that description is accurate." Brandon casually stated while making small circles with his thumb on her knee.

"I should have said something to you." Dahlia was looking down while still facing Brandon.

"It was better that you didn't. If you had, she would have just made you out to be jealous. With our history, I would have only believed it if I saw it for myself. Which I did. Thanks to Dorian for convincing me to meet up with him for drinks that night."

I turned and looked up at the man sitting on the armrest of the couch that I am sitting on wearing a devious smile, which lets me know he knew exactly what he did that day.

I redirected my attention away from the always casually topless and overly entrancing he-devil and back to my brother. "I didn't know she cheated on you. You just said that you guys grew apart that night at the bar?" No wonder why she was so pissed and Brandon was beaming with relief.

"We had grown apart. Honestly, we should have ended things long ago. I just didn't want to hurt her. I never felt like i could be my true self with her. Things worked out the way it should have in the end."

Brandon didn't hide his grin as he watched Dahlia as she was leaning forward to pour herself another drink.

Brandon slapped his hands on the top of his thighs as he abruptly stood up. "Enough about that. I'm glad you're home. I'm going to go back to my place and take a nap before I have to get back to work. You joining me, Dee?"

"Nap my ass." Dorian mumbled under his breath.

Dahlia smirked at her twin before turning to Brandon, widening her smile, "As if you have to ask. I'll talk to you later, Shonnie."

Making myself comfy on the long sofa, I flicked on the television going through our streaming collection, choosing a movie at random to watch. It hasn't escaped my notice that Dorian has remained here with me, not speaking. He has slid off the arm of the couch to sit on the cushion, maintaining a reasonable distance from me. We remained that way for the entire movie, quietly staying on our designated sides of the sofa. I kept my eyes on the screen, never turning even the slightest in his direction. I could feel his eyes on me every so often, assessing my mood, waiting for an opening from me. A part of me wants to give him that opening, give him that chance to make me swoon for him.

My mind drifted, and I wondered what it would be like to give him what he wants. To let him have his way with me. I shouldn't allow such thoughts into my mind. I'm dating Adrian and he's amazing.

Yet still, it wouldn't hurt to get to know my best friend's twin brother. They're obviously close, and I don't want things to feel uncomfortable when we're all together.

"So, would you like to pick something to else to watch?" I continued watching the screen filled with movie stills, scrolling aimlessly.

When he didn't respond, I turned my head to look at him. That was a mistake. I don't know how i forgot that he was wearing nothing but a pair of loose, very thin, dark grey pajama pants. He's just lounging back topless, with both arms thrown over the back of the couch. An invitation, I'm sure.

Dorian is a work of art. Those tight rippled abs on his lean frame would make anyone froth at the mouth.

Once my eyes finally stopped their appraisal, I looked into those gorgeous amber eyes of his. Dorian arched a brow in curiosity. He reached his hand out towards me, and I placed my hand into his. We both remained silent and my eyes lingered on his as he continued holding my hand firmly, making soft caressing circles with his thumb against mine.

Breaking the silence, Dorian says, "As much as I hate to ruin this lovely moment, I would need the remote to choose our next movie."

My eyes widened as I comprehended his words. I tensed and tried to pull my hand back, but Dorian stopped me, gripping it tighter.

"Don't do that. Luckily, I have two hands and multitasking is second nature to me." I relaxed and handed over the remote. He quickly dropped it into his lap and reached over, placing his free hand lightly on my hip, encouraging me to scoot closer to him. I obliged, appreciating the comfort he was offering. I wasn't even aware I needed until now. I leaned into his side as he wrapped his sinewy muscled arm around my shoulders. He continued to astonish me when he chose a romantic drama. One of my favorites. A Cinderella retelling with a historical setting. Half way through the movie, I unconsciously cuddled closer into Dorian, leaning back on his chest. His arms are now holding tightly around my waist.

"You know, you and her are very similar." His reference to the main character made me curious about his meaning.

"Why? Because her name is Danielle and mine is Shontelle?" I snickered.

"I hadn't even thought of that. Besides that, it's your love of the written word. Your insatiable thirst for knowledge. Your breathtaking beauty that you don't even seem to be aware of, that isn't only skin deep. Not to mention your incredible strength." Each word from his mouth squeezed at my heart and sent butterflies soaring through my stomach.

I held onto his arms, hugging them close to me. We remained like that for the rest of the movie and long after it ended. "Tell me something about yourself that no one else knows, with the exception of Dahlia. She is, after all, your twin and there for a part of you."

"I'll share if you promise to share something with me as well. Same concept, something no one knows." Dorian countered.

I nodded in agreement and smiled when he held up his pinky. He chuckled when I happily wrapped my pinky around his and shook it hard.

"I don't think Dee knows this but, when I was a teenager in high school I tried to convince our parents to allow me to homeschool. I couldn't handle all the attention. They convinced me to continue. They felt that I had to learn how to handle the adoration, and I did." I looked up at him. His eyes were on the blank television screen. "My junior year, One of my teachers stalked me. No one knows how far his obsession actually went. Let's just say I didn't come out of it unscathed. So after they arrested him, I visited him to confront him. I lost my temper and told him he should just do me a favor and kill his self. Two days later, I found out he did exactly that."

I sat up to look at him, and he dropped his head, looking at his lap. I cupped my hands around his cheeks so that I could look into his warm pools of gold. "You can't blame yourself for the decision someone else made. You were just a kid, and you had every right to be upset and try to get closure. It wasn't your fault." He winced at that last part and sighed.

"Either way, that day I learned to watch what and how I said things."

I pulled back started up when I realized I was still cupping his face in my hands. I pulled my legs up under me and sat on my heels, still facing him with my eyes lowered. I let out a deep sigh. "It's my fault my dad is dead."

Dorian looked at me, stunned, but remained silent. Patiently waiting for me to elaborate. "When I was twelve, I drove a wedge between my parents and they separated because I was being a selfish brat. Two years later, after couples' therapy, they were going to reconcile. I was grateful. I was always more of a daddy's girl before everything happened. The night my dad was supposed to move back home with us, my siblings and I planned a surprise welcome home party. He never showed. My mom tried to contact him but she never got a hold of him. Hasn't been seen since. After he was declared deceased, I shut down and isolated myself from everyone because even though they wouldn't say it, aside from Julissa, i knew they blamed me for fracturing our family."

Dorian gently held and squeezed my hands in each of his. They looked comically small in his. He gave a weak smile. "I hate to be a plagiarizer, but you can't blame yourself for other people's actions. There's no way you could have known how things would play out. I don't believe your parents would hold you accountable for their actions."

"The guilt still weighs heavily on me because I miss him so much every damn day and I'll never get the chance to apologize to him or tell him how much I love him." I sobbed as Dorian pulled me into his embracing arms. He held me as if i was the most precious thing in the world.

"No matter what you've done, your father loved you. It would be impossible for him not to. Loving you is as natural as a heart beating and as easy as breathing. To not be able to love you would be like suffocating." My pulse raced rapidly at his declaration. Even though I knew he was only trying to console me. My breath caught as he placed a chaste kiss on my forehead. I raised my head slowly. My eyes lingered on his mouth for a moment. Dorian's arms, still cloaked around me, loosened slightly as I leaned in gingerly, pressing my lips to his. His lips moved leisurely against mine. My hands glided up his neck into his soft curls, as i parted my lips for him as we both simultaneously tried to deepen the kiss. It was as if we needed to consume each others breathe to survive. A sudden knock at the door broke us from our trance. We both fought to catch our breath. I gradually stood up, refusing to look away from what has to be sex in its physical form. Another knock forced my eyes towards the door.

"I better see who that is." Dorian didn't move from his seat. I opened the door just enough to address the person at that door. My heart skipped, before beating rapidly as I looked up into two grass green eyes.

"Hey beautiful, is everything alright?" Adrian asked.

I tried to keep the guilt I was feeling from my face. "Yeah, I'm just tired and trying to process everything that has happened in such a small amount of time." I casually inspected the hall, finding my bodyguards each positioned at the stairwell and by the elevator.

"Brandon told me you were back home, so I just wanted to stop by to check on you before I headed out to take Cassandra to the airport." My heart sunk. I feel like a complete asshole. I tried to give a reassuring smile. "If you're up for it, i'ld like to take you out to lunch tomorrow?" Adrian asked, as his hands ran up and down my sides in a soothing gesture.

"I would love that. As long as you don't mind having two extra bodies trailing behind us."

Beaming with the most priceless smile, Adrian leaned in, placing a soft kiss on my cheek. "For you, I would sit in a kennel with two rabid wolves. I'll be here at noon to pick you up." The stupid butterflies are back, wreaking havoc in my stomach as I watch Adrian walk away.

I closed the door after turning back inside, my guilty conscience must have been plastered all over my face. Dorian met me half way disappointment and something else i can't quite pinpoint on his face.

"You should get some rest. It's been a long day for you." His eyes wouldn't meet mine.

"I'm sorry, I shouldn't have…" cutting me off, Dorian placed his hands on my shoulders.

Sighing deeply and letting out a silent curse, his head tilted upwards. "You have nothing to be sorry about. You did nothing I would want you to take back. Despite the situation, I hope you don't regret any of it, because I definitely do not. I'll be here anytime you need me." With those words freed, Dorian retreated to the guest room.

My heart was still beating erratically. I hurried into my room, flopping face first into the stack of pillows. I need to sleep and hopefully I can pull my shit together in the morning.

22

The thick clouds that are threatening to spill copious amounts of rain and, thanks to my luck, plenty of thunder and lightning with a very darkened sky. All the ingredients for a meeting between a dark sorceress and a gentle knight. That's all I need is another date gone wrong with this gorgeous man.

Wrapping his thick muscular arms around my waist, pulling me close with my back to his front. Adrian nuzzled my neck, causing goosebumps to spread all the way down my chest. I shivered as he kissed the sensitive skin between my neck and collarbone. "What's the matter Sweets, afraid you'll get wet?" He joked as he pulled open the restaurants door . Little does he know, around him I am always drenched. Well, my panties definitely were.

We'd gone out to my favorite sushi restaurant and all I've been doing is salivating over how sexy he licks his lips.

After we finished our meal, Adrian's hand squeezed my thigh as he turned my stool so that I faced him with his knees on either side of mine.

We've been spending almost every day together since I've returned home. After my moment of weakness with Dorian, I questioned if I should tell Adrian or just act as if it never happened. I obviously chose the latter.

Dorian has been avoiding me by staying out all day, every day and most nights. I guess he just went back to his old habits. It's probably for the best. After our moment i couldn't shake the feelings that i felt growing for him. So the separation is good, I suppose.

"So, what should we do next? Going home is not an option. You need to get out and let your beautiful curls bounce free." Adrian proclaimed, breaking me from my wayward thoughts.

"Really, because I think that this is perfect weather for cuddling under my thick fleece blanket, watching movies and snacking." I told him as I wrapped my arms around his neck, encouraging him to go in for a kiss. Thankfully he obliged me.

"How about we go to the movies and cuddle in there loungers while eating whoppers and extra buttery, artery clogging popcorn?" Adrian proposed.

"Sounds amazing." I agreed.

We decided to watch the latest action and humor filled, comic book adaptation. Since it's still early in the day there aren't any patrons in the theater. Just my security duo, that found separate seats on both sides of the theater in front of both exits. Giving us some privacy.

Half way through the film my mind began to wander, making comparisons to my life and the characters. Gifted with powers to protect the ones they care about. The hero or maybe more of an anti hero, has to be guided by others to make better decisions so that history doesn't repeat its self ensuing chaos.

I wonder if that's what's going to happen with my family. Will history repeat itself and my mom suddenly just disappears without a trace? What about me or my siblings?

What if one day my gift does evolve on its on and I can't control it and it consumes me? The possibilities of my mental capabilities developing into something powerful like telepathy or telekinesis is unfathomable. What if I can't control the amount of memories I intake and develop some type of psychosis. What if my mind implodes and I'm left a blubbering mess.

"Hey Sweets, what's wrong? You're trembling." Adrian breaks through my small mental panic attack, pulling my slimmer frame tightly into his hard, with just a hint of softness, body.

"It's nothing, I just let my thoughts run a little bit too far." I confessed.

Adrian slid one off his hands down to my hip, the other wrapped around my shoulders holding me close, as I cradled my head in to his neck. Our height difference isn't a hindrance as we're reclined in our seats with the dividing armrest up. The soothing smell of leather and citrus makes me cling to him.

Adrian's hand slides up and down the back of my thigh as he massages the muscles there. I pull my head back to look into those gorgeous emeralds that seem to shine even in this dim theater.

Adrian leans in with a ghost of a kiss on my lips. His hand now tightly gripping at the base of my ass. I reach up sliding my fingers into his coal black hair gripping lightly as I try to deepen the kiss. Our tongues dance, as our mouths try to combine our souls.

Adrian breaks the kiss long enough to redirect his lips to behind my ear, sending shockwaves down my spine. My arms wrap tightly around his torso, my hands push into his muscular back. Holding tightly molding my body to his.

As he brings those perfect pink lips back to mine, Adrian simultaneously glides his hand back and forth, from my bum to my snatch. The friction ignites a heat wave in my core, that leaves me senseless.

"Do you like that, Sweetheart?" Adrian asked in a husky voice I barely recognized.

"Mmhmm" I whimpered as I pressed my core into his. I began grinding myself against the bulge tightly pressed against his zipper. Holding on for dear life as Adrian's hand moved in between us and I felt the warmth of his palm sliding down my belly into my leggings past my panties.

I moaned softly into his neck as those long thick fingers perused through my soaked slit.

"You're so wet sweetheart, am I going to have to take these off so that we don't ruin them?" Adrian whispered in a rough strained voice. My thighs clench together as pressure continues to build deep in my core. My breaths are labored as Adrian's fingers continue to play with my now swollen nub. As I writhe helplessly beside him, not caring that I'm in a public place. Somehow knowing I'm in the darkened theater and can be seen at anytime only excites me more.

A gasp escapes me as Adrian dips a thick finger inside my dripping core. My body, and mind, shatters as an explosion of sheer bliss and pure pleasure surges through my entire nervous system. My body goes slack as I try and regain my wits.

Once my vision clears and I'm able to regain my focus, I look up into Adrian's lust glazed eyes. His devilish smirk sends a cool chill down my spine.

Keeping his now, more Jade then emerald, eyes locked with mine as he pulls his hands from my pants and brings his fingers into view. My wetness visible even in the dim theater. He slowly sucks my juices from each finger.

Hot lava resurfaces in my belly and I lose all sense of sanity. I dive in and capture his lips with mine. Coaxing him to open for me with my tongue. My mind spirals as I taste my release on his tongue, all I can think about is the pleasure he has ignited that is now spreading like a wildfire through my entire body.

Adrian grips one of my breast through my thin sweater and gently squeezes. My peaks began to harden and strain against my bra, begging to be freed.

"I think…. We should…. go." I gasped, in between kisses.

"Are you sure?" Adrian asked, his breathing rapid as I trailed kisses down his jaw and neck.

"Absolutely." I needed to get him home and in my bed, now.

"If that's what you want, that's what we'll do." His voice deep and sensual.

We both stood up abruptly, after quickly adjusting our clothing, we walked hurriedly towards the exit closest to us. My guards moved instantly as they saw us retreating from the theater, both searching for threats begging us. I guess our abrupt evacuation triggered them.

I giggled as Adrian guided me quickly to his car the anticipation filling me with excitement.

The trip home was short and sweet. Adrian held my hands the entire ride. Luckily the hybrid Mercedes he drove today could practically drive itself. Another perk was the spaciousness of the interior that filled my mind with all types of naughty thoughts, I'll store those away for another day.

Wrapping his arms around me as soon as we stepped into the elevator Adrian pressed his soft lips to the base of my neck. Gently guiding my loose curls away from my shoulder he kissed, licked and sucked at my sensitive and heated skin. Never once breaking contact as we slowly made our way to my door. I hastily unsecured the locks.

Wasting no time, Adrian pins me to the door with his powerful body. I gasped, excitement and arousal driven adrenaline coursing through me as our mouths clashed and our hands roamed over each others bodies. My top and sweater were the first to go bunched together and thrown carelessly to the floor. Adrian's mouth trailed down to my perky, plump breast that are practically spilling from my confining bra. My head fell back against the door as I felt the warmth of his mouth close over my peaks. His tongue lashing at the hardened tips of my areolas. My fingers played in his hair massaging his scalp as he squeezed both breast together. His tongue licked across both of my breast. Quickly removing the oxygen stealing garment I grabbed Adrian's hair softly pulling his mouth back to mine. My hands reached down to the hem of his t-shirt and pushed it up his torso not missing an opportunity to run my hands across his thick sinewy muscles.

Adrian pulled away to relieve himself of the garment. My heart skipped as I took a good look at his gorgeous soul stealing beauty. This man should be carved in stone, forever remembered in history.

Reaching out I drag my fingers lightly across his chest, taking in every detail of his frame. At this moment, I am grateful that I'll never be able to forget this.

Adrian lifts my chin with his index finger so that we are looking eyes to eyes, " Are you okay Sweetheart? If this is too much we can slow down."

"No, it's just. I'm happy that I'll have this memory of you always." I whispered.

"You'll have more then just the memory, you'll have me always. No matter what happens, I'm yours." Adrian said gently. Before he placed a gentle kiss on my lips.

Grabbing both of my hands he walked backwards towards my bedroom.

Catching me off guard Adrian swiftly lifted me by my waist and wrapped my legs around his hips. As I held on to his neck he opened my room door and froze immediately.

My instincts immediately put me on high alert.

"What the hell are you doing in here?" Adrian growled.

My head jerked towards the direction Adrian was staring. Standing in front of my en-suite bathroom in his favorite clothing option, a towel, was Dorian. His hair wet and dripping around his shoulders, body glistening with perspiration from the shower. His body's muscles perfectly defined against his lean frame.

My body turned half way towards the man that never fails to shock me with his stubbornness and carefree nature. Our eyes locked, his gold trying to penetrate my silver. I was entranced.

"I do believe I asked you a question." Adrian hissed. Breaking my mind free from his beautiful compulsion. Dorians eyes drifted down and one of his brows rose slightly questioning. Realizing I was completely topless Adrian pulled my body into his blocking Dorian's perusal.

"Come on Now, I'm just leaving from a refreshing hot bath. I don't want too cause any problems I'm just trying to relax. If you want I can sit quietly in the reading chair and just watch." Dorian's mischievous smile is priceless as he teases us. If he is just teasing.

"It would be best if you just left." Adrian proclaimed, stepping aside so that Dorian could exit.

Once he is directly in between us and the door, he leans over to Adrian and whispers, "I thought you loved to share with me."

My eyes widened in astonishment as I stared at Dorian's sexy as sin, retreating back.

Lowering me to my bed, Adrian shakes his head. I knew then that the moment had ended. Wrapping my arms around my chest, I became self conscious and stood up, grabbing one of my oversized hoodies from my chair and threw it on.

"You should get some rest and I'll talk to you later." My Adonis said as he placed a chaste kiss on my forehead. I stood there stunned and disappointed. After a moment I followed Adrian out of my bedroom. I paused in the doorway just in time to see him shove a semi dressed, still topless, Dorian into the wall. "I know what you're trying to do. It's not going to happen again so back off." Adrian hissed.

Not missing a beat Dorian, gave him a roguish grin, before giving his retort. "Oh, I don't know it just might. I mean your time is already limited and you'll have to figure something out."

Adrian steps back freeing Dorian, shaking his head, " I know." Was the last thing he said before leaving the condo.

23

After spending two weeks with me on lockdown, Dahlia decided we needed a fun day. I have finished all of my required classes and I'm just waiting for graduation at the end of spring, even though I already have both of my doctorates and a stack of job offers.

I tried to invite Adrian to join us, but he had a lot of work to oversee at his newly renovated house. Dorian was more than willing to join us. I couldn't exactly deny him. Dorian has continued to be tender and attentive towards me. Not to mention protective. Although, the antipathy between Adrian and Dorian has become suffocating. After the last verbal altercation between the rivaling Step-siblings, I'd opted to meet up with Adrian at Brandon's place.

He moved home a few days ago to be make sure his final renovations were as they should be. Things are getting more serious between us, but it feels like Adrián is holding back, or possibly hiding something. I have to admit Dorian has also been vehement about his affections for me.

So, of course, we're going to go to Hollywood for the day. Get our theme park on and walk down Sunset at sunset. That's the plan. I opted out of wearing matching colors like the twins, but I kept it cute and casual with some navy leggings, an oversized white button-up shirt with a dark grey waist belt and grey knee-high, flat boots. I pulled my black curls up into a high ponytail. I kept my makeup simple thin black liner and mascara, with a sparkling gold dusted gloss for my lips. The twins are wearing dark denim pants and red button up tops. Dahlia tied hers above her midriff with the first few top buttons open, showing a hint of cleavage. The red complimented their bronzed skin and golden eyes. She too opted to keep her makeup light and natural with her hair cascading in soft, dark brown waves down her back. Although they both are ridiculously attractive, they remind me of thing one and thing two from the cat in the hat. Especially when they're bickering amongst themselves.

"Let's do the Transformers' ride next." Dorian suggested.

"I vote we take some pictures, or find something to eat." Dahlia countered.

I have watched them go back and forth like this for the last hour. Just as I started to intervene, I heard a loud female voice call Dorian's name from behind me. We all turned to see a young Latina woman coming our way. The same woman he had brought to the condo after drinking himself into oblivion a couple of months back. She walked straight up to Dorian and grabbed his neck and dived in for a very sloppy wet kiss. Dorian's face turned to me and looked perturbed. The disgusting sight lead Dahlia and me to walk off towards the nearest food stand.

"Does he even try to control himself, like ever?" It irritated me knowing how easily he could have anyone he wanted. Men and women all swoon over him. I know it's not any of my business, but I think he deserves more.

"I wish. It would definitely make my life a lot less dramatic. Albeit, it can be entertaining on some occasions." Dahlia chuckled before continuing. "I know it may be hard to believe, but most of the time, it's not entirely his fault. Now and then, he might give in just because keeping others at bay is harder for him. People have always gravitated to him, even when we were babes. In high school, he was a king. Every girl wanted him and some guys, and the others wanted to be him or close enough to reap the benefits of being around him."

"Sounds like a gift and a curse." I acknowledged.

"For him, I would say curse. Someone has definitely proven it to be both. Junior year, a stalker almost abducted him. Turns out his history teacher, ironically, had an entire future planned for the two of them. Luckily, he was so obsessed with him he couldn't refuse him when he asked him to take him home and to stay away from us. According to Him the teacher became overwhelmed with physical pain when he tried to refuse his wish to be taken home and left alone."

Before I could ask her more about what happened, Dorian sat at our table by the food stand, his irritation clear. Dahlia's phone chimed, and after checking it, she turned to me. "Brandon just texted me. He's here by the main entrance. Don't fret, he ditched his security detail, and he didn't know that you were here with us. I'm going to go get him." She was gone before she finished her sentence.

"If I knew this would be an outing for couples, I would have invited Adrian." I mumbled to myself, not at quietly as I thought.

"Careful Love, as beautiful as you are, green isn't your color." Dorian mocked.

"Your implication of me displaying any form of jealousy is hilarious. I couldn't careless what pet you waste your time with. I just don't want to be the odd man out." I reached inside my bag in search of my phone, only to realize we left it so I would appear to be at home.

As if reading my thoughts, Dorian holds his phone up with a taunting grin on his face.

"Would you like for me to call the man of your dreams for you?" Before I could give a response, he put his phone away and looked mischievously into my eyes, "I would rather not, since I know he's just another annoying nightmare." He scoffed before adding, "Not that it's any of your business, but we are not a couple. I didn't even know she would be here."

"Who's looking green now?" I taunted. Dorian slid closer to me on the curved bench, throwing one leg over the side and turning his body so that his front faced the side of mine. He leaned forward in to me so close that I could feel the warmth of his breath against my cheek. His chest is so close I almost leaned in closer to him.

"I could make your dreams and fantasies a reality. All you have to do is let me know when you're ready to be mine, and I will give you everything you need and more." My heart is beating so fast that I'm afraid it will burst right out of my chest onto the table. These men are going to make me need a cardiologist. Fighting the overwhelming urge to grab him by his wavy black hair and kiss him until my mouth is the only thing he can think of, erasing every other person he has ever kissed from his memory.

"As enticing as that sounds, unfortunately, the line to ride you appears to be endless." I derided.

He gently places a hand on my cheek, slowly turning my head so that I look at him dead on. "I'm offering a frontline pass just for you."

I scoffed.

"Who has a frontline pass and why haven't we been using it?" Dahlia implored. as she plopped on the bench next to her brother as mine sat next to me. After straightening his back but remaining by my side, Dorian continued to observe me as if I were the most fascinating thing in the park.

"You know that our mother is going to lose her mind if she finds out you're not at home." Brandon lectured.

"Maybe you should call her and let her know that I'm safely hanging out with my big brother and my friends in a very public setting." I suggested.

"Did you somehow forget you were kidnapped at a party full of people?" His sarcastic question had a point.

"No one was paying attention to me." I noted.

"I beg to differ." Dorian mumbled to himself.

"I don't want to focus on any of what happened. Let's just get on the world famous studio tour." I suggested.

Although I somehow ended up on a double date left me paired with Dorian. I enjoyed every moment from the tour to the stroll down the Citywalk. when Dahlia and Brandon would venture off, Dorian stuck to me like glue while keeping me entertained. He told me about his childhood pets and his hobbies. When he opened up his phone to show me, I was astonished to see his artwork, from sculptures and oil paintings to coal sketches and street art. It was beautiful and powerful. There was so much depth and dimension. I felt as if he had allowed me to take a peek into his soul. This new perception of who he really is has left me floundering. Is he attractive? Absolutely. Does sex permeate out of his pores and saturate through my core? Undeniably. Would I risk my heart and soul being shattered just to have him all alone and to myself for one night, filled with passion and pleasure? I'm indecisive, but leaning more and more towards yes with each of our encounters.

"Margaritaville will be our last stop." A slightly disheveled Dahlia announced. Saving me from my impervious thoughts.

"What do you want from me, Dorian? Scratch that, never mind."
I'm sure I know exactly what he wants. What I can't confirm is
whether I'll give it to him. Too much tequila equals bad decisions
that I am currently all too ready to make with this gorgeous man
before me.

"Relax Princess, I'm just trying to go to bed. Since my sister is
bunking with your brother, I want to make use of the free bed." He
assured me.

"Don't call me princess." I warned with a slight slur. "Why can't
you sleep on the couch in the family room?"

"I don't want to be close enough to hear them bumping uglies."
Dorian confessed.

"Fine." I conceded. "I hope you don't snore."

"Don't worry, I don't, but I have been known to growl, and it
makes most women purr." He relayed that information with an
actual growl that sent a shiver down my spine and a throbbing pulse
between my thighs.

"Just keep your animal instincts to yourself tonight." I
commanded.

"I'll try, even if it's against my nature." he giggled.

We crashed at one of Brandon's friends' home that is currently
out of town. Opting to be on the safe side, since we all drank way too

much. One twenty-minute Uber ride later, here we are. I feel like I'm trapped in both my worst nightmare and my wildest fantasy. Okay, maybe not my worst nightmare, but a nightmare none the less.

"I refuse to follow you blindly. Just because our parents want us to work together doesn't mean that's something I would ever agree to. This is a perfect example of why. Your superiority complex. I don't work for you. You're not my superior." Adrian turned, giving Dorian his back.

"I tried to be civil and communicate with you. I allowed you to make your own decision of your own freewill which apparently was a mistake." Dorian's words come out casually, but there is an undertone of malice.

Adrian turned to him with a look of disgust. "Your so-called alpha bark doesn't work on me. So, what is your plan, to talk to me to death?"

"Now I understand why you got demoted from the fierce ones squad. You don't pay attention to the things that matter." Dorian leered at Adrian.

Adrian pushed Dorian into a wall, pinning him in place with his forearm pressed against his neck. "You know nothing about me and you never will. Just because our parents made their decision doesn't mean I agree. Once we find her, I'm gone. I wanted nothing to do with this shit." He seethed before releasing his hold on Dorian.

"We are in this because of you. You did this. You let her get taken. You abandoned her when she needed you to protect her. So you better find her or I'll show you I can do a lot more than just speak pretty words." Dorian shouted towards Adrian's retreating back.

My heart was pounding rapidly in my ears, my body engulfed in perspiration. A cold chill lingering throughout the room. Yet, my entire back is flushed with heat. A strong arm covered in sinewy muscles enclosed around my ribs and another under my head. The warm breath at the base of my neck caused the tiny hairs there to rise. Dorian's scent of cashmere and sandalwood, with a hint of tequila, wafted over me.

I let out a small whimper when he unexpectantly pulled my body into his, cradling me into him. My back pressed firmly into his chest and my ass to his alarming erection. The sheer size caused my breath to catch. Whoever argues that size doesn't matter obviously hasn't felt this monster. Heat quickly built in my lower belly and I clenched my thighs together, trying to hold back the building pressure. The small movement causing me to brush against his arousal, which made it twitch. My breath went still in my chest.

"Don't worry, you can breathe. I won't let my Dragon out to play unless you beg me to." The husky bass in his voice vibrated against my neck and in my ear. He chuckled as a shudder rushed through my body, straight to my core.

"Why exactly are you in my bed?" I whispered, my voice catching as I tried and failed to relax.

"You wouldn't stop thrashing around and you kept saying my name. You called to me so I answered your call." Dorian explained, adding emphasis to the obvious innuendo.

"Dorian, you know that I'm with Adrian. I have no plans to be another reason for you guys to be at each other's throats. You guys are even at war about me in my dreams, only they play out like you both are actually in the center of a war." Dorian's body went stiff behind me. Maybe I shouldn't have mentioned Adrian.

"Never mind, I'm going to the bathroom." I shimmied myself free from his perfect warmth to free the tequila that had overstayed its welcome in my bladder. When I returned, Dorian had a haunted look on his face that vanished the moment he saw me.

"Are you okay?" I asked in a soft whisper. I wasn't trying to bitch at him.

"I'm fine. Can we just go back to sleep? I promise to keep my hands off you." I slid beneath the thick comforter and arched my body into his. Once I was settled, I simply reached behind me and pulled his arm back across my waist. Despite how much I try to fight it, I can't deny the feelings that flood my system just being near him. I know Adrian is the perfect guy for me, but what if Dorian is as well?

Taking that thought as permission, my hips rotated slowly, grinding into Dorian's now semi hard erection.

"You might want to consider trying to be still. Before I allow my dragon to take control." he warned me. His husky voice laced with lust.

I stopped my slow grind, only to grab his hand from my waist and guide it up to cup my full breast. With no further encouragement necessary, his other armed moved down too. He cupped both of my breast gently, tweaking my nipples between his fingers. His lips pressed a soft kiss to the nape of my neck and another to my collarbone. Each touch caused my heart rate to spike in my chest. Dorian slid his tongue up from my collarbone to my earlobe, nibbling on the latter. My pulse was now thrumming between my legs. I pulled my bottom lip in between my teeth as I clenched my thighs together, trying to contain the flood gates. My hips once again are rolling of their own freewill.

I let out a low moan as one of his hands explored more of my body as the other continued kneading and teasing my breast.

With one hand under my rib and the other gripping my hip, Dorian whispered in my ear, "Tell me to stop and I will stop right now." His hand gradually sliding down to my thigh, squeezing lightly. I turned my body to face him. Responding with my lips on his.

"Please, don't stop." I panted against his mouth. Whatever restraint he had was gone instantly. His kisses became feverish and dominant as he took control.

Reaching back, I simultaneously ran my hands through his

thick and silky waves and wrapped my calf firmly around his. He rewarded me by squeezing my arse with one hand before slipping his fingers through my slit into my wetness, holding my head steady as he devoured me. I pressed his hardness to my drenched core, and I rocked against it, loving the friction. I gasped as his hand snaked between us and he rubbed my clit in tiny circles. I could no longer contain the volume of the moan that ripped out of me.

"Fuck, you look like a goddess made just for me when you're about to cum. Don't hold back Angel, cum for me."

His fingers moved faster, his tongue warm on my throat. My body shivered. Dorian's mouth closed over mine, consuming the scream that broke free as every nerve in my body went haywire. His fingers slowed and his whole hand rubbed gently against my throbbing core. My legs are shaking and I can't seem to catch my breath.

"Slow, deep breaths, Angel. Take your time." He removed his hand from my soaked cunt, causing me to let out a small whimper.

"I'm sorry." I breathed out. I nestled my head under his chin.

"Why are you sorry? You came so beautifully. I may not have an eidetic memory, but I promise you, I will never forget this moment or any that are with you." My heart tightened in my chest and I had to calm my breathing for a new reason.

"We don't have to stop. I just needed to catch my breath. I have little experience with physical pleasure. I didn't know my body would do that."

"I think it would be best if we both get some sleep. If you still feel the same when we're both completely sober, we can do whatever you want back home. Where I can take care of all your needs properly."

Not knowing what to say to that, I nodded. Turning over and readjusting back to our starting position, it only took a few seconds for me to drift off.

25

After everything that happened between us, I'm surprised that Dorian is the one sleeping like he's comatose. I maneuvered myself from the bed and his alluring temptation. It's early morning. The sun is barely rising. I found my clothes and quickly dressed. I look over to the bed and my core heats to hot lava. Dorian is laying on top of the bedding wearing nothing more than boxer briefs. He's still laying on his side and his back looks just as impressive as his front. Muscles ripple down his back. He definitely puts in work for his body because that ass can not be natural, it's too perfect. It's too biteable and I'm getting a craving. I sigh deeply before forcing myself out of the room. Resisting that man is my biggest struggle. I guess that's why I gave in so easily last night. I don't regret it, but I'm glad he stopped it before it went too far. Which is another thing to shock me. Looking back, I realize I judged him too quickly. He deserves a chance to show me the real him, but what about Adrian?

I make my way to the kitchen to search for some coffee. Fortunately, I don't have a hangover, just in case the others aren't as fortunate. I'll have some ready for them as well. I turn on the television while I wait, keeping the sound low. I flip through a few channels before leaving it on the news. It couldn't hurt to catch up on current events the old-fashioned way.

Brandon comes out of the room with a serious case of bed head and a look of pure bliss. I look at him knowingly and he smirks. He pulls at my curls playfully before grabbing a mug from the cabinet.

"Hangover?" I ask.

"No. You?" He leans back against the sink.

"Nope." He stares at me with a knowing look. As if he is waiting for me to say something more.

"Just ask whatever you are going to ask. You obviously have questions for me."

I sipped my coffee before looking down the hall to the spare room and then back to the door he just came through. In a low whisper, I asked him a question that has been burning through my mind, "What's your gift?"

He looked at me, bewildered. "Umm, what do you mean, exactly?" His body shifts slightly with unease and he runs his fingers through his wavy onyx hair.

"Mom, didn't tell you I knew?" I asked.

"What is it exactly that you know? What does she know?" Brandon's face contorts with confusion.

"Wait, I'm confused. You don't have any special powers?" He's making me perplexed.

"Do you have special powers, because Julissa doesn't?" My brother asks.

"Yes, I do. That was the whole reason they kidnapped me. I just hadn't known yet. Mom never told you what happened?" I inquired. The befuddled look on his face was answer enough. "Do you even know how we got this way?"

"What can you do?" He asked, turning my question on me and ignoring the other.

"I asked you first."

He grinned and then rolled up his sleeves right before he said, "This!"

Then he threw his hands up in front of me, and they erupted in flames. I jumped back on instinct, slamming into the refrigerator, trying to get some distance from the blaze displayed before me.

"No, fucking way! How the hell can you do that?" I gasped, trying to remember how to breathe.

"I don't know how to explain it. I'll try right after you tell me what you can do?" Brandon declared.

"Nothing as awesome as that. I can see people's memories. Sometimes I feel like there's more I can do, but I don't know how to unlock it. Occasionally, I think I get stuck in their dreams or memories. Sometimes, I can't differentiate between dream and memory."

"So, you can read minds?"

"Not exactly. I can only access the memories and store them with mine. I can't hear active or past thoughts."

"Have you tried?"

"Of course not. I don't even want to have this so-called gift. I can't tell reality from fantasy and if some memories I've seen are real…." I stopped speaking as soon as I heard the bedroom door open.

"Good morning, loves." The Zombie, formerly known as Dahlia, rasped as she made her way to the coffee, scratching at her perfectly knotted bed hair. "How come you two don't look like shit?" she inquired.

"Good genes, I guess." Brandon quirked a smile.

Dahlia looked at him with a raised brow and snorted. "Lucky you."

I gave Brandon a look that said this wasn't over as he pulled Dahlia's body in to his. Her eyes searched the living room.

"Where's Dorian?" She inquired as she took a sip of her coffee. Trying to keep the guilt off of my face, I tilted my head in the direction of the second bedroom.

"Sorry about last night, Spyce. I thought my brother was going to sleep on the couch. Since that's where he was when we went to bed."

"Don't worry about it, it's not a big deal. We should head out, though. I don't want my mom to freak out."

"She knows you're with me. I let her know yesterday." Brandon explained.

"Thanks for that, but I still would like to get home. I want to see Adrian." "Why? Do you need to compare his garter snake with my Dragon?" Dorian whispered into my ear as he crept up behind me.

My soul nearly jumped from my body. I turned to face him, our eyes locked. Those beautiful golden eyes burrowed into my core, sending a wave of lust through me. He gave a devilish grin. His hands are lightly placed on my hips. His shoulder length hair is silky and hardly out of place. I licked my suddenly dry lips and his eyes focused on my mouth and he groaned. I forced myself to move away and went to watch the news.

"This morning SILA announced a new threat right here in the United States. They claimed that there are terrorist cells hiding right under our noses. We'll have more for you on that story at seven, but first in entertainment Julissa Spyce made the cover of most of the tabloids this morning after some very raunchy photos were leaked of her and a new guy getting very intimate in a popular restaurant by the pier."

"What the fuck! There's no way that's real." Brandon proclaimed.

My body turned to lead as I sunk back deep into the sofa. My mind not actually processing the image on the screen of my older sister Julissa sitting on Adrian's lap at the restaurant he took me to on our first date. She has her arm wrapped around his neck and is leaning in as if she's waiting for a kiss. My stomach feels like it's tied in Shibari knots to my heart. Someone turns the tv off and then Brandon is in front of me.

"Shonnie, you already know that when it comes to tabloids, nothing is really what it seems. So before you get upset, maybe you should talk to them first."

My brother is always optimistic. I'm more of a realist and i follow the evidence.

"I'm sorry, love, but if I saw that photo and you were in it, I would probably bury you alive in my garden." Dahlia declared to Brandon. After giving her an arrogant look, he turned his attention back to me.

"Shonnie please, before you get upset, get the facts first."

Is this my karma for what happened between me and Dorian? I mean, I initiated it. Hell, I even pushed for more and wouldn't have stopped if Dorian hadn't pumped the brakes.

"It doesn't matter. Let's just go home."

We took an Uber back to Universal Studios parking lot to pick up Dahlia's car; then we made our way back home. To avoid Los Angeles gridlock traffic, she took back roads.

My mind refused to focus on anything other than the photo now permanently seared into my brain. The betrayal was painful. The only problem is I don't know who's the true betrayer. Julissa has always had this need to make everything between us a competition. She couldn't match me intellectually so she always tried to one up me with simple things like clothes, friends' parties and so on. Any time something good happened to me, she either stole the attention or ruined the moment. When I graduated high school and college the same year, she convinced my mom to throw a huge party, knowing that I didn't want one, and then made sure no one I knew was on the guest list. After my first date, Julissa snuck out and slept with him and then sent me the photos. She claimed to be testing his commitment to me. On my twenty-first birthday, she made plans to get me drunk and leave me in Cabo Saint Lucas, fortunately Brandon was with us and ruined her plans. Everyone thought she was just going to make it a prank, but I knew better.

I watched the water as we moved up the coastline. The forever winding road of the Pacific Coast Highway was relaxing as I watched the surfers riding the early morning waves. Dahlia and Dorian were bickering about their short-lived trip to Europe in the front seats. Brandon sat quietly beside me, watching me cautiously. He's probably trying to figure out what's bothering me the most, our family's hidden secrets, or the publicized betrayal. It's an easy tie between them both at this moment.

"Adrian wants to talk to you about the pictures." Brandon spoke softly, as if he didn't want to startle me.

"It's unnecessary, the pictures said enough." I mumbled, keeping my attention on the waves.

"Shonnie, I really don't think things were as they seemed. Plus, you know how Jules can be." The statement ran true but, the compromising photos were hard proof of his indiscretion, with my sister none the less.

Brandon placed his hands on my shoulders, turning me to face him. "Adrian is not the type of guy you think he is." He implored.

"Correction, Adrian isn't the type of guy I thought he was." I admonished.

He stared into my eyes as if there was more he wanted to say, but held his tongue.

"What aren't you telling me, Brandon? Did you know about them?"

His hands dropped from my shoulders into his lap. His eyes searched mine as if I should have the answers that he refuses to give me. I focused in on him, trying to find what he's hiding that he thinks I should already know.

"You really should reconsider straightening your hair, Shonnie. I mean, these curls are out of control. I guess you just have more of dad in you than the rest of us." Julissa chastised me as she tried to detangle the mess on my head.

I ignored her and continued to read my book. She looked up at our brother and then over to his friend that she gave a look of disgust to as he fed his pet rat at the breakfast nook in the kitchen.

"Why does he always have to bring that rodent here? That's disgusting. We eat at that table." She declared.

I looked up at the brown and white rat that was obviously clean and well cared for, and shook my head at her absurdity. I looked at the long and skinny boy with shaggy strawberry blonde hair and green eyes and he smiled. His eyes moved to my sister and lingered before he got up to move towards us. Julissa screamed before taking off, stumbling over the back of the loveseat to get away.

"One day I'm going to make your sister crazy for me" He laughed, to my brother.

"Good luck with that." Brandon scoffed.

My eyes blurred with the tears that I refused to let free. I turned my attention back to the beach. My body abruptly jerked to the side as it slammed into Brandon's shoulder. Dahlia screamed violently as she tried to control the now spinning out-of-control vehicle. It slammed harshly into the side of a black delivery truck.

"Dorian, wake up!" Dahlia screeched. He groaned as he slowly pushed her hands away, that were slapping him in the face. I looked up into my brother's green eyes that currently has a reddish orange hue around the outer ring that I've never seen there before.

"Brandon?" I squawked as I watched the gash on the side of his head bleed freely.

"I'm fine Shonnie, what the hell just happened?" Brandon asked, exasperation in his voice.

"This jackass just clipped me and tried to kill us!" Dahlia shouted, her rage seeping as she tries to free herself and her brother from their seatbelts. I undid my own as I moved myself away from Brandon, trying to better assess his damage. He's covered in blood from his head wound, but it looks to have stopped its flow. A stocky tanned man about my height with greasy dark brown hair opened my door and peered in. I flinched away from the unexpected interruption.

"Are you guys okay?" Good samaritan asked. "My friend called for an ambulance. Here, let me help you out of the car." I allowed him to help me out slowly.

I looked around at the extent of the accident. We're pinned in between a common black SUV and a black delivery truck. Another man was standing by the SUV on the phone yelling in another language I didn't catch. He's probably trying to shift the blame away from himself. I looked back to see if anyone else was being helped, only for the man helping me to become more aggressive as he continued to lead me towards their vehicle. I struggled against him as he opened the vehicle door. My survival instincts took over just as the pretend good samaritan lifted me off the ground from behind, trying to force me into the vehicle. I slammed my head back, hearing the crunch as I broke my would be captor's nose. He cursed as he dropped me, losing his balance. I immediately swept his legs from under him, knocking him on his ass. His companion made his way around the front of the vehicle, coming straight for me. I took off running as fast as I could in the middle of the highway, away from the accident, searching for someone to help me.

The highway was empty of any other vehicles. I cursed myself for leaving my phone at home, trying to avoid being traced. Hopefully, my brother called for help. I fell to the ground as I heard and felt an explosion behind me. Flames completely engulfed the black SUV and my pursuer was lying on the ground in front of me, not moving.

Brandon was jogging towards me. He stopped in front of the man, laid out on the asphalt and lifted him by his suit jacket with one hand. While pointing a flame lit index finger into the man's face. I wasn't close enough to hear what he was saying. I made my way closer, catching the man's response.

"They'll never stop hunting her. She will never be free. She's too much of a risk. She will either join us or die. They will never allow her to live to be used against us. She's a weapon and they want her and so they will have her. Do your worst hot hands." The look in my brother's eyes made the man recoil.

"Fire isn't my only talent." Brandon smiled at the man just before he threw him into the dirt on the side of the highway as if he weighed no more than a pebble. He walked over, stopping directly in front of him, placing his hands in the dirt. I didn't understand what I was seeing. It was impossible. The man sank as the dirt rose and covered his body as he was lying on the ground with a look of shock and undeniable fear. His body was completely buried with only his mouth and nose exposed.

"Shonnie, let's go. We need to get out of here before their reinforcements arrive." Brandon shouted at me. I was frozen in astonishment.

"How the hell did you do that and how do you know they'll have reinforcements?" I asked as he pulled me out of my shock and we made our way to the mess of vehicles. The delivery truck driver was laid out in the middle of the road, completely unconscious, with a wicked looking black eye and busted lip. His body was covered in shrubbery and vines.

Dorian and Dahlia were standing by a blue four-door Nissan sedan. They both appear to be unharmed, but have dried blood on them in different places. We all loaded into the car, Brandon in the driver's seat, Dahlia in the passenger and Dorian in the back with me. Brandon took off with haste. Speeding well above the limit all the way home.

No one uttered a word as we continued our way home. The eerie silence filled the car with tension.

Dahlia broke the suffocating barrier of silence. "Brandon, I don't think we should go home. They might track us somehow."

"Don't worry, they can't right now." He showed her something I couldn't see from behind his seat. Whatever it was, it took away some of the worry from Dahlia's face. Not knowing what to say, I looked out the tinted windows.

My mind was a mess of confusion and paranoia. Every passing vehicle became suspicious. Even the birds flying overhead made my brow furrow with worry.

"Ignatios has been gradually adding more guards to my detail and around our building, so im sure we'll be safe once we return." I announced to the car.

"Once we are secure inside, I'll contact everyone that needs to be updated on what just happened?" Brandon added.

"I hope you consider the police in the need to know group." I proclaimed, redirecting my attention away from the window to the rear-view mirror. Looking into my big brother's eyes that couldn't seem to figure what color they wanted to be.

"No, I don't." Brandon declared.

"I must have missed something. Why the hell not? Do you

suddenly have beef with the PO PO?" My voice rose slightly as I teased him, my voice heavy with sarcasm, curiosity, and frustration.

"I have my reasons. The only one you need to understand is that we're trying to maintain our anonymity and the 'PO PO', as you call them, has no problem leaking valuable information to the highest bidder. So no, we won't be contacting any form of law enforcement. Our family is more than capable of handling things on our own."

His point was valid, but my irritation at being out of the loop of all of our family secrets is still simmering below the surface. "You're right. I just hate not having all the information. I'm left with an uncertainty about how to proceed from here. You, better than anybody, know how hard it is for me to be left with only speculation and no verification. My mind will wander and leave me to my own devices."

"I know, and that is why I won't leave you to speculate. We'll talk as soon as it is safe to do so. I'll tell you everything I can." His voice was sincere and I trust he will. I can't help but notice his undertone and that he said he will tell me everything that he can, not everything that he knows.

Brandon parked the stolen car in our building's underground structure in an unassigned parking spot. An older man from our security team that I've only seen once or twice patrolling the building approached our group as we were vacating the vehicle. Brandon met up with him before he was in earshot. Their conversation was short, and together they made their way towards us. We continued to make our way towards the elevator. Brandon caught up to us. The guard diverted towards the vehicle, opening the door and getting in to the driver's seat. He revved the engine just as the elevator doors opened and we all stepped in. During the ride up, we agreed to get cleaned up and handle our personal needs, then meet up in twenty minutes at Brandon's place.

28

My knee bounced erratically on its own as I sat on the edge of my chair. Normally when I hang out here, I would melt into the soft plush of the thirty-five inches wide winged back. Reaching over the small end table that divided the twin seats, Dorian placed his hand at the top of my knee, giving it a faint squeeze. I settled and looked over at my brother. Despite everything that has happened, he isn't the slightest bit rattled. He is completely calm. Dahlia walked out of the kitchen, handing out waters to each of us.

Brandon sighed heavily as he started off the overdue conversation.

"Shonnie, I'm going to need you to listen to me without interrupting. I will give you a chance to speak. Just let me get everything out first." I nodded in confirmation, and he continued. "Our family secret isn't only our family's secret. There are others like us. When our parents left their jobs with the department of defense special ops team, their whole team left with them. There was some discord amongst them about what their next steps would be. Everyone involved had been exposed to the experiments. Some believed they should start a pharmaceutical company to further their research to cure terminal illnesses and others wanted to use their 'Gifts' as you call them, for more nefarious purposes. Which later would cause in house conflicts. Since our parents were the original projects, lead scientists, the others looked to them for answers. Our father decided that those who were against moving forward with only the affordable pharmaceuticals company should leave. Which they did. Only to resurface two years before you were born as *SILA*." He paused. Looking me over for a reaction. I was definitely having one, but I picked my jaw up off the floor and shut my mouth. When he was sure I would stay quiet and just listen, he continued.

"The pharmaceutical company was thriving, and no one knew that the newest active terrorist group were their former colleagues. After two of the scientists and a member of the company's sales team disappeared without a trace. Our dad investigated. He never found them, but he discovered that they each were last seen with the same former colleague. When the sales team leader resurfaced, dead as a Christmas tree on Easter. Our parents got spooked enough to dismantle the company and all the original team members went into hiding." He concluded.

"So, mom knew about the people coming after me?" I asked, astonished and trying to wrap my head around this information.

"No, she didn't because they shouldn't even know you exist. Julissa and I were babes at the time, but you weren't even in the oven yet. Also, you were sort of a miracle no one else could procreate after the first three years of their genetic transition and mom had you five years later." Brandon conveyed.

"So wait, none of them could have children?" I asked, disturbed by the terrible side effect of my father's experiments.

"They could and they did, just not after those first three years." Brandon assured me.

"Do you know if SILA killed dad?" I worried my lip trying to contain the tears that are threatening to spill free.

"I can't give you the answer to that. Maybe you should have that conversation with mom." He told me. Once again I noticed his careful wording.

"Have you talked to her? Does she know what happened today?" I questioned him. If he has, I'm surprised she's not here with a full militia ready to drag us to the family manor and implement a complete lockdown.

"I did, and she does. Which brings me to our next move." Brandon sighs deeply. "Mom wants us to get out of the country. She has family members that live in Sicily and Romania. It's up to us to decide which we want to stay with."

"What the hell, I can't just leave! I just got my doctorates and I don't know these people. Plus, wouldn't we be putting them in danger by being there?" My voice breaks, and I'm sure I'm about to have a panic attack.

"Shontelle, calm down and just think. Mom has disappeared before she knows what's the best way to stay off SILA's radar." Brandon tries to reassure me. It doesn't.

"You don't know that for sure. It's possible that Dad was the one that kept us off their radar and now they found us because he's gone and not coming back!" I was becoming hysterical. My eyes were flooding with tears of frustration. Brandon pulled me into his arms. He embraced me as I fought to pull myself together. "I miss him. I need him here more than ever."

He remained silent, just holding me until my breathing evened out. "Go home and get some rest and when you're ready, pack a light bag, only what you absolutely need that can't be replaced. You won't need your passport or any form of identification, so don't bring anything that identifies who you are."

I gave a curt nod before turning to Dahlia. I forgot she and Dorian were here. "What about them? If we've been under surveillance, they can be in danger as well."

Dahlia gave a weak smile, that I think was meant to be reassuring. "We're coming with you guys. Technically, we shouldn't have been on this continent, anyway." I gave another nod and made my way to the door.

Dorian caught up to me as I waited for the elevator. On the ride down, he finally spoke. "I know what you're planning and it's a bad idea." I kept quiet as I unlocked my door. He continued. "It's better for you to be on the run with friends and family than alone, with no one watching your back."

I froze in the middle of the living room. "Are you some type of psychic? How did you know that was what I was thinking? Are you one of them? Is that your power?" I drilled into him. He just stared at me with astonishment adorned on his face. "No, to all of that. I'm just observant and I pay attention to you. I heard your concerns, and I know you are more than capable of doing anything you set your mind to. Two doctorates, two masters, all completed by the age of twenty-two. You're obviously more than capable."

"I appreciate you saying that. It means a lot to me. Now leave please." I Said.

"What? No." He said.

"It wasn't a request." I proclaimed.

"I don't care what it was. I'm not leaving you." Dorian declared.

"Well, too bad because I'm leaving you. All of you. I'm the one they're actually after. I won't risk anyone I care about. Just go back to your wonderful life as a philanderer and I'll go back to being invisible." I advised.

He stepped into me, brushing a loose curl behind my ear. "You've never been invisible to me. For me, you've been a beacon guiding me to where I really want to be. Not even the night could completely hide the Moon." I took a small step back and turned to my room. I need to get out of here before he convinces me otherwise.

29

"So, what's the plan, Spyce? You're just going to run off and disappear into the wind alone without a clue? No, fuck that. I'm going with you."

Refusing to look back at him and those eyes that glow like stars, i say, "No Dorian, you're not! I will not put more people in danger while I'm being hunted like a wild mare."

Dorian lets out a condescending chuckle and says, "I don't recall asking for your permission. You shouldn't be alone. Plus, I've traveled more than you and I know how to disappear in to the wind if necessary."

His declaration is just another reason I'm mildly suspicious of him traveling with me. I barely know him and what I know isn't bad, but it's also very curious. He has always seemed protective of me or possessive, depending on how you look at it. I enjoy his company. I just can't imagine being alone with him and not being possessed by him. The way he's willing to just up and leave and follow me to the other side of the world, literally. It warms more than just my heart. Maybe I need to just accept the fact that I won't be able to resist him. I truly don't want to be completely alone in an unfamiliar country, hiding and trying to not be kidnapped or killed. "Alright, you can come."

"I must admit I was expecting a little more fight and don't worry,

Angel, I'll make sure you come too." He smirked in that disturbingly mischievous way only he could. I'm already regretting my decision. "Make sure you only pack the bare necessities and we'll make a bank run, but only for cash. One withdraw before we go to make sure that we don't have to use our cards. They can be traced and we don't want to leave a trail. We have to become ghosts in the wind," He informed me.

"I guess I already saved us some time." I informed him as I slid over my nightstand and opened my floor safe, revealing the contents inside.

"Should I even ask why you have what looks like half of a million dollars hidden under a Catwoman nightstand?" Dorian asked, his eyebrows reaching for his hairline.

I just shrugged my shoulders. "My dad always taught me to plan ahead. You never know what day will be doomsday." I wiped at the tear that escaped.

Dorian approached me as if he could sense the anxiety building inside of me. He pulled my shaking hands into his own. He softly rubbed small soothing circles around my wrist. Looking into my eyes as he said to me, "You're going to need to trust me and listen to my directions. You will make it through this. I'll make sure you're not found. I'll make sure you're safe. You will always be safe with me. You will also come back from this stronger and wiser. Which I can guarantee."

My heart thumped rapidly in my chest as he pulled my body into his. His warmth and masculine smell of pine and cashmere overwhelmed my senses, sending a great need straight to my core. I looked up into his amber depths that shined like two golden orbs reaching for my soul. Feeling lost and helpless to heed their call, I took a step back, only for him to move with me, sliding his hands up and down the sides of my waist. I was no longer retreating. I was being guided closer to my bed.

"Why are you so adamant about helping me?" I asked in a low whisper, almost to myself.

"I'll do anything if it will bring you peace and keep you protected." His response broke my resolve.

"Your so beautiful, it should be a sin." He smiled at my words and my breath caught at the sight of his perfect teeth and lips.

"Sweet girl, I am Sin and you are my guiding angel." Dorian whispered softly into my ear as his lips brushed gently across my jaw.

I slowly wet my lips with my tongue. He caught the movement and leaned in, gently brushing his lips across mine. I didn't hesitate and kissed him deeply, tilting my head to give him more access. His tongue slid across my lips, begging me to open. I couldn't deny him. He consumed me as his hands roamed down my back, cupping my cheeks. My arms wrapped around his neck, keeping his mouth on mine, refusing to separate for a moment. Dorian lifted me by my thighs and I wrapped legs around his waist, feeling his need for me grow between my legs. Wrapping one arm around my waist, he removed my top as he maneuvered us onto my bed. Lying me gently on my back, he sat back on his heels with his knees between my thighs. Dorian removed his shirt and my arms reached out on instinct, my hands traced each rippled muscle on his torso. His hands roamed softly over my breast, kneading and squeezing. He tugged gently at my nipple before tracing over it with his warm, wet tongue. Sending Heat straight to my molten center. Dorian's mouth left a trail of wet kisses down my stomach.

With expert precision, he quickly removed my pants and continued his exploration with warm kisses and teasing nibbles on to my thighs. I jerked up as he pressed a kiss to my now drenched thong. That showed how desperately I needed him. Dorian looked me in my eyes as he slowly dragged the tiny strip of fabric down my legs and placing them in his pocket. My head fell back onto the small stack of pillows. I gasped in surprise and a needy whimper escaped me as I felt his tongue delve into my core. He lapped at the mess between my legs vigorously before sucking my clit into his mouth.

My body trembled as I felt the warmth of my impending orgasm building into an inferno. Perfectly latched on to my bundle of nerves, Dorian slid two fingers into my pulsing cunt and my body erupted. Without pausing, he continued to pump his fingers into me with precision, working me through the orgasm. Once my body stopped its tremors, Dorian removed his fingers from my soaking wet heat and sucked them clean. Licking his full lips that glistened with my release.

My body shivered with pleasure. Dorian moved with a quickness, removing the remainder of his clothes. My body was buzzing with anticipation and excitement. Spreading my thighs wide, his body hovered above mine. I looked down at his long, thick erection and my eyes widened and panic took over me. "Don't be frightened. He's a friendly Dragon." Dorian teased, his voice low and husky. "He just wants to give your body what it needs. Now relax for me, Angel." I did as i was told. He guided his tip to my entrance, sliding it through the slick wetness seeping from my slit, before entering me slowly. Dorian looked down into my heavily hooded eyes. His own filled with raw, hot passion. Threading his fingers in between mine, he stretched our arms above my head. His thrusts were slow and penetrating deep. I cried out as he stretched me. I shivered, feeling the power of this man's strength as his hips slammed into mine. Pushing both of my hands together to hold them with one hand, he used the other to raise my knee, pressing it high into my chest. This new angle was more intense as he fucked me deeper and harder. He muffled my loud screams by capturing my mouth with his before it escaped my lips. Once my screams turned into moans, Dorian spread his kisses down my cheek to the sensitive spot of my neck below my ear. I could feel the sensational pressure building in my core. The friction against my clit from his deep grind with each thrust was pushing me over the edge. I felt the tears slowly slide down my face towards my ears. We were so close that not only were our bodies joined, but it was as if he was trying to merge our souls. My release dragged out a cry that felt like my soul was shattering. He kissed my tears Slow and deliberate.

Dorian raised up just enough to lift my hips. He increased the speed of his thrust as I felt the warmth of his tongue on the peak of my breast. "Dorian, please… I can't…. please." I didn't know what to say. I was delirious.

"Fuck, Angel, you feel like heaven and I never want to leave." Whatever feelings I may have been fighting for him, I lost that battle stupendously. This moment will forever be seared into my memory, stocked with the best of them, and I will cherish it always. It might also cause an obsession, a dangerous addiction that I'll never get enough of. "Don't worry, Angel, I'm going to take good care of you." His voice was breathy. He ran his tongue softly down the valley between my breast kissing and teasing them both while thrusting deep and rhythmically. His teeth grazed my peaks one at a time before I felt his deliciously warm mouth close around one. He knows exactly how to work that tongue. Every kiss, every touch, every breath was perfect. Everything felt natural, as if my body has always belonged to him, almost as if we had done this before.

I closed my eyes and just allowed myself to take it all in. The way he smells, the way he tastes, the feel of his lips and hands all over my body. The sounds He made. I don't know how, but Dorian has to be the mystery guy from my first time, my special night in ecstasy. It's almost exactly the same, just not in a dorm room on a twin sized mattress.

My eyes flew open and widened as i looked up into those liquid honey eyes. "It's you, you're the one."

He smiled. "I'm glad you think so, because you definitely are the one for me. Now come again for me, sweet girl." His thumb gently circled my bundle of nerves and his thrust became more intense, harder and deeper. I ruptured, screaming his name, my body tightening and gripping his length. Dorian leaned over, gripping my hips and pounding erratically as his release spilled deep inside me. We both fought to catch our breaths.

As impossible as it may seem, I think my mind is playing tricks on me. Then again, I could just have a case of wishful thinking. I feel like I should feel some inkling of regret, but I don't. Everything happened so organically, it was as natural as breathing.

As the euphoria died down, betrayal etched at me. Adrian, what will he think of me now? Giving in to my baser needs with no thought out consideration. I don't want to lose him, but I also don't want to drag him in to my mess. Dorian has followed me down this path into the unknown black abyss. I hope once this is over, maybe he'll understand that this wasn't personal, and leaving with Dorian is circumstantial.

Yeah, I highly doubt I'll be able to convince him that's true. I can't even convince myself. Dorian pulled me into him with my face to his chest, holding me close. "Talk to me Angel. What's going through that brilliant mind of yours?"

How could I confess my thoughts to him after what we just did? I'm an asshole. I shouldn't be thinking about Adrian at a time like this, plus he betrayed me with my sister, maybe. I should have talked to him and gotten his side. It's too late. I'll be gone before he gets back. "Just thinking about what I'm leaving behind."

Dorian squeezed me closer into his body as he whispered into my ear. "Don't stress yourself with things that are beyond your control. There will always be plenty of issues. That doesn't mean you have to take them all in or carry them alone. You only get one chance to live your life. So live it to the fullest and live it for you." He chastely kissed my temple before climbing out of my bed. "Plus, you can change your mind and I'll get you to your family." He added before making his way to my en suite bathroom and starting the shower.

Returning to my room, he grabbed his boxer briefs pulling them on. "Get showered and packed to go. I'll do the same. We will leave as soon as you're done." I nodded, and he left my room after quickly dressing. I wasted no time doing what I was told.

After I was done, a loud rumble came from my stomach. I rushed into the kitchen, grabbing one of Dahlia's meal prep containers. She won't mind. Lamb curry over a bed of brown rice with a side of broccoli. I placed the container in the microwave and set the timer for three and a half minutes. I made my way back into my room, grabbing my already packed small overnight bag from my favorite clothing store, my Harley Quinn back pack that is mostly filled with cash and the smaller toiletry bag that came with the overnight tote. Bags in hand, I left my room and placed them at the door. I shouted out down the small hall to Dorian that I was ready. I turned to make my way to the kitchen to retrieve my on the go meal. Only my body froze as I became aware that Dorian and I weren't alone in my condo.

Sitting at my small dining room table was a tall and muscular giant of a man with a bald head and dark ebony skin that looked as smooth as silk. Staring at me with silver-gray eyes. His attention diverted from me to Dorian, whom just walked up and stood beside me.

Almost as if on instinct, Dorian stepped in front of me, hiding me from view of the stranger. As our uninvited guest stood up, looking directly at me, Dorian growled as he stepped forward, his fist balled at his side. The man didn't even flinch as Dorian made his intentions clear. Moving quickly, I stepped out in front of him, cutting off any potential act of aggression towards either man. Turning away from the confused look on Dorian's face, I looked up into the pale sterling silver eyes of a ghost.

"Dad?"

ABOUT THE AUTHOR

Living in Southern California with her kids and overactive imagination, she decided after being on lock down in 2020 to work on publishing her novels she wrote a decade prior. Writing has always been her passion and now she wants to share that with anyone that enjoys reading as much as she does.

Printed in the United States
by Baker & Taylor Publisher Services